The Glass Tree

The Glass Tree

Michael J. Manz

ENDICOTT STREET PRESS
BOSTON

For Mom and Dad

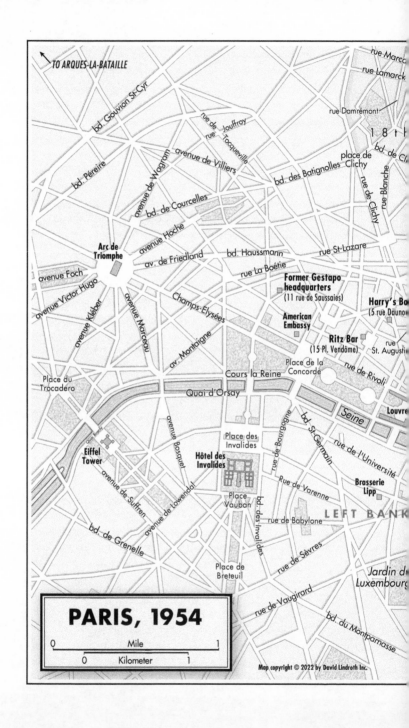

TO ARQUES-LA-BATAILLE

rue Marc
rue Lamarck

rue Damrémont

rue de Jouffroy
rue de Tocqueville

bd. Gouvion St-Cyr

18 t

place de
Clichy

bd. de Cl

avenue de Villiers

bd. des Batignolles

rue de Clichy

rue Blanche

bd. Péreire

avenue de Wagram

bd. de Courcelles

avenue Hoche

rue St-Lazare

Arc de
Triomphe

avenue Foch

av. de Friedland

bd. Haussmann

rue La Boétie

Former Gestapo
headquarters
(11 rue de Saussaies)

Harry's Ba
(5 rue Dauno

avenue Victor Hugo

Champs-Élysées

American
Embassy

avenue Kléber

avenue Marceau

av. Montaigne

Ritz Bar
(15 Pl. Vendôme)

rue
St. Augusti

Place de la
Concorde

rue de Rivoli

Place du
Trocadéro

Cours la Reine

Quai d'Orsay

Seine

Louvre

avenue Bosquet

Place des
Invalides

bd. St-Germain

rue de l'Université

Eiffel
Tower

avenue de Suffren

Hôtel des
Invalides

rue de Bourgogne

Brasserie
Lipp

avenue de Lowendal

Rue de Varenne

bd. de Grenelle

Place
Vauban

bd. des Invalides

rue de Babylone

LEFT BANK

rue de Sèvres

Place de
Breteuil

Jardin d
Luxembourg

rue de Vaugirard

bd. du Montparnasse

PARIS, 1954

0   Mile   1

0   Kilometer   1

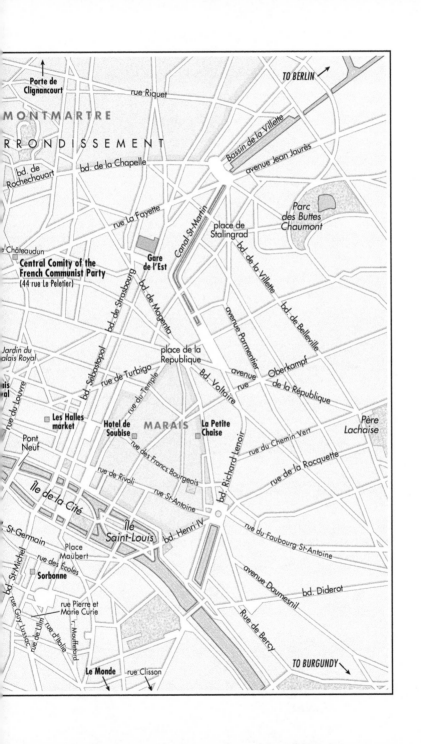

PARIS

May 1954

Chapter One

JEAN-PAUL TOSSED HIS PACK OF CIGARETTES on the table and pulled out a chair. I hadn't seen him in a year. He was the same bull of a man. Maybe a bit grayer, but still a wrecking ball in plumber overalls.

"You look like crap," he said, flipping up his lighter and striking the flint.

He leaned back, stressing the chair and turned his gaze to the street and then the other deadbeats sitting at Le Carré Rouge. I went back to my newspaper and Pernod. I probably did look like shit. I was developing a gut and hadn't shaved since being put on *unpaid* leave. Any day now I'd be dismissed and sent back to the States.

Did anyone at the Embassy even know I was part of Eisenhower's "Stay Behind Army"? Somebody must, I thought. Lot of good I'd be when the Ruskies marched into Paris.

And now my father-in-law, or whatever you call the father of your dead wife, was sitting across from me smoking and looking like he wasn't sure whether or not to say what he'd come to say.

I folded the paper.

"What's happened," I asked in French.

JP held out his pack of Gauloises and I took one. I liked

the French cigarettes even though I got Lucky Strikes at the Embassy. He pushed the lighter across the table.

"I need your help on something," he coughed. "It'll be an hour of your precious time."

This last bit he said with a wave of his hand to encompass the café and maybe my life in general.

JP had all but blamed me for Liana's death the last time we spoke. Protecting her was my only job as a husband, he'd said. And now he wanted a favor. I pushed away the old hard feelings and the urge to tell him to "fuck off." A year ago I hadn't been so restrained.

"What do I have to do?" I asked.

"I need to collect a bill. It might get rough."

"Don't you have pals in the Union for that?"

"I just need you at the door. I don't want him to run."

I gave him a dubious look.

"It's sensitive. I need family."

JP's eyes held mine a moment and then looked away.

Family?

As far as I was concerned, the funeral had marked the end of whatever kind of family we'd been.

"I'm touched Jean-Paul, but I don't break legs for a living."

JP stabbed out his cigarette. "Just meet me here at 3:00. Can you do that?"

"Okay, fine," I said. I didn't want him to start throwing tables around.

He took some francs from his pocket and tossed the coins on the table.

"And take the day off," he said, glancing down at my glass.

4

I felt my blood boil and gripped the table to keep my temper.

"Courage," he muttered as he reached the sidewalk.

I stood up, stunned by the word, and after leaving a few more francs, headed off in the opposite direction. I didn't stop until I reached the stairs to the Seine.

The first time Liana had asked for "courage" from me was before we were married. I could picture us, standing naked in the cold stream behind her cousin's farm in Burgundy.

"Will you love me *courageously*?" she'd asked.

I remembered the smell of the pine trees that grew sideways down to the riverbed and the deep pool under the cliff.

And lacing my fingers to hold her tight.

"Will you always love me?" she asked, leaning her head back to study my eyes.

"Always," I answered.

"Avec courage?" she asked, her brow furrowing. "I mean, will you love me courageously?"

I said I would even as I wondered what she meant.

We toweled off and then lay in the sand.

"You've made it so I owe you my life," she said. "Sometimes I wish you hadn't."

Liana turned on her side and pressed herself against me.

"I love you for saving me, but I would have left, Eli. You know that, don't you?"

"You don't owe me," I said.

She turned my face to hers. "No one's ever made me feel so wanted, so quenched, so believed in. It's amazing to feel so much love. But it scares me too, because — that's not me. I'm not like you..."

That night, back at the quiet farmhouse, I listened to her breathing as she slept and wondered how I'd ever need courage to love her.

At 3:00 p.m. I headed back to the café and found JP waiting on the curb. I followed him down rue Bonaparte.

He moved fast even with a limp that I hadn't noticed before. It was too warm for the sweater I'd worn but I didn't take it off. Some part of me was glad to see another spring in Paris. But I knew if I let it be more than a vague thought it would be ruined. Liana had loved this season too.

I almost asked JP about Liana's older sister, Alix. I'd seen her a few weeks ago standing in a doorway with a man dressed like an American gangster. Her hair was very short, like it was cut in prison, and she looked thin and sickly.

Instead, I asked after the youngest. Emilienne.

JP grunted. "She's back in Florence to be with her mother."

His voice was full of disappointment. Shortly after Liana died, her mother had moved out.

All JP's women left him.

We could have crossed the street and walked through the park but JP led us along the tall black fence until rue Auguste and then turned left.

"We're close," he said.

We were only a minute's walk to where Liana was gunned down two years ago.

"JP," I started.

"I know where we are, it's just coincidence."

He took us down another block back toward St. Germain, which made no sense at all, and then hooked right.

The buildings here were narrow and two stories. This was a neighborhood for professionals and bureaucrats.

"Just stay at the door. Don't let anyone in and don't let him get out."

I noticed then that JP was carrying a leather satchel, something a professional pool player might use to keep a stick.

"I don't want to be part of anything violent. I'm sure you could just have his water turned off."

"Just stay at the door and don't get involved."

When we came to the street where Liana had been killed I stopped in my tracks.

"It's just a street," JP said. "People still live here."

I felt my hands go cold and my heart race. I'd only been here once, to see where it happened. There had still been blood on the sidewalk.

JP pulled me beside him and walked on. I felt like we were trampling sacred ground. At a black door in the middle of the block JP stopped and knocked. It was answered a half minute later by a man in his 30s in a black turtleneck sweater and green corduroys.

"We are here about the kitchen faucet," JP said.

"There's no problem," the man replied, taking off his glasses and wiping them with his undershirt.

"Philippe Garnier? 68 Curie? Your landlord reported it I suppose."

"Yes, but…"

"I'll need to see it to sign off," JP said, like the cog in the system he was.

He turned to me. "Stay here, Ferrand."

I nodded.

The man opened the door for JP and I stepped into the doorway before he could close it.

"C'est une bell journée," I said.

He nodded and I thought maybe I recognized him — but from where?

He followed JP out through the back. From the vantage of the doorway I surveyed the clutter of books, records and instruments. A long coffee table with journals and newspapers sat in front of a comfortable-looking leather couch. An ashtray attached to a standing lamp overflowed with cigarette butts. This guy clearly wanted to show how hip he was. I noticed the framed pictures on the bookcase when the man returned in a hurry and out of breath.

"Out of my way," he said, striding to the door.

I took a step in his direction and he veered behind the table. Now JP entered from the back and the man practically snarled.

"Leave this instant!" he demanded.

JP looked over at me and nodded toward the door.

I looked out into the street and shrugged back at him. "The coast is clear," I said in English.

The cornered man froze and looked at me with sudden recognition and horror.

JP unzipped his bag, pulled out a police truncheon and put his wrist through the leather strap.

Philippe considered his odds of rushing the door and then thought better of it and unexpectedly sat down on the couch.

"I need a cigarette," he said.

"Too bad," JP spat. "Now tell me everything that happened or I will crush your fucking skull."

I took another step inside. What the hell was going on?

The man took a butt out of the ashtray and lit it with matches from his pocket. It took him another half minute to talk.

"She was here," he said, looking down at his cigarette. "When she left I heard the shots. I went to the door, a car was just turning at d'Ulm. I went out to her, but... she was already dead."

He looked up at JP and then stubbed out the butt. "The man, Osval, was choking on blood. I held his head. 'Why?' is all he said."

I felt numb. I might have fallen over if I hadn't reached for the doorframe.

I heard JP ask him about the car, if he had moved anything, why he hadn't told the police. But I couldn't follow anything, the blood pounding in my temples deafened me. I couldn't breathe and suddenly felt sick. I stumbled outside and felt vomit rush up. I spat and sucked air and took deep breaths until the confusion turned to a surge of rage. I went back to the door and charged in.

"You fucking asshole!"

But JP was ready for me. His vice-grip on my arms pushed me back outside. And then I was weak again.

Jean-Paul brought me home in a cab. The buildings along the way were blurry and red. He came up the stairs, went into the kitchen for a bottle of whiskey and sat me down on my bed like an invalid.

"I'm sorry you had to find out like this," JP said.

He either took my key or left my door unlocked because an hour later Alix was holding my hand and shushing me like a baby. I was drunk enough to think she was my Liana, somehow come back from the dead to comfort me now that her secret was out.

In the morning Alix was still there. Still in the dress she had come over in and lying next to me on the bed. She must have been out somewhere when JP found her and sent her over. Why? Because he cared that I'd just had my guts kicked out? Didn't he know this would happen?

By the time I pulled myself out of bed Alix had made coffee, eggs, toast and ham steak. I suppose she thought I still ate like an American or that I could possibly have an appetite.

She sat across from me at the table eating a croissant and jam. There was only a faint resemblance between her and her sister. The same small mouth, dirty blonde hair. I noticed that hers had grown back some and that she was looking healthier. She looked at me with green eyes, Liana had blue.

"Papa told me what happened," she said in French. "What a bastard."

"How did he know?"

She turned to look out the window. "I had to go away a bit. Papa went through my stuff. He found Liana's letter."

"No offense, Alix, but why would she tell you about an affair?"

Her gaze returned to my eyes. "I was surprised too. It was the first time she'd treated me like a sister since the war. She had wanted to apologize, or what passes for an apology from Liana. I suppose we were now equally despicable in her eyes."

She poured herself some coffee and blew over the top of her mug.

"I thought you knew, Eli. Liana said something about a letter she wrote you. But she never did?"

I shook my head. "I never saw it."

"It's awful I know, but I thought I had my sister back. This little secret of hers. She told me she wanted to stop. She loved you. She loved you more than any of us."

I couldn't even laugh, my head was aching from the whiskey. I held my head in my hands instead of eating. My mouth felt as dry as parchment.

She seemed to know what I was feeling. "I gave you a sedative last night. You were tossing and turning, moaning like a kicked dog. You needed sleep."

"Thanks for coming over," I managed.

"You're still my brother," she said, patting my hand. "In-law." She smiled.

I nodded and felt myself crying again. I let it come. I let the tears shake me even as Alix wrapped her arms around my chest.

"None of this is your fault. None of it is. Liana was not easy."

I stopped crying and wiped my face with the napkin Alix had set. "How long did it go on?" It mattered somehow.

"I don't know. Truly."

"I want to know. I want to know it wasn't always."

"It wasn't," she said, sitting down again. "The letter came only a few months before she died. I sensed it had been a recent thing. Something she was ashamed of."

"Then why? Why did she do it?"

Alix took my hand on the table. "Probably nothing to do with you. She was what, twenty-two when you met? A student. You were her savior. She grew up, and she's French," she said with a twist of her lip.

"She could have told me."

"What's to tell?" Alix replied. "I have to go. You'll be alright?"

"Do I have a choice?"

She gathered her purse from the bar, taking out a vial and leaving it on the table.

"Why are you still here, Eli? Why aren't you home?"

She gave me a look, a slight turn of her head, and then closed the door behind her.

I'd asked myself that question a thousand times since Liana died. Why not just leave this place? The people, every café, every street reminded me of her.

But I wanted to spit on the grave of whoever had done it, whoever it was that ruined my life. I stayed to see them hang. Then after a year I doubted anybody ever would. The suspects they brought in, militant communists, all had alibis, the party leadership insisted they had nothing to do with the killing. But nothing else made sense. Osval, the target of the gunmen, had a rap sheet a mile long for thumping communists. He'd been a collaborator of the worst kind during the war.

The Sûreté called Liana collateral damage. A bystander walking by at just the wrong moment.

Why she had been in that part of the Fifth was not known. But it was close to the Sorbonne where she taught. She was thought to have just been out for a walk. Now I knew why.

My friend in the French SDECE could ask questions in ways the Sûreté could not. But he pointed the finger at gunmen from Russia who came and went and were now likely lost behind the Iron Curtain. The CIA agent I met with told me the same thing.

JP hadn't liked it. Didn't believe American or French spooks knew any more than the police. He must have kept at it. Hadn't given up. Didn't let himself fall apart.

I knew I'd hear from him again. Maybe it would be a couple days. Time enough to stay drunk. I picked up the vial Alix had left. Little white pills. I unscrewed the top and shook one into my palm. It was my fault. I had lost her somehow. What had I done? I went to my bedroom, opened the closet and took down the ammo box where I kept Liana's letters from after the war. They fell onto the bed as a group, tied with a pink ribbon. I knew I hadn't done that. I undid the ribbon and went through them one by one. Liana had put them in order from first to last, but there was nothing else. No confession.

The first time JP came around he let himself in and stood over the bed. I knew he was there. I knew what he'd see too. I was giving myself over to misery. I didn't want to live. I didn't want to die but I didn't want to exist anymore. I just wanted to disappear.

Alix had been back too. She took the Miltowns and replaced them with something stronger, something that let me drift away. I didn't even think. Not about Liana, not about sleep, not about anything. When they were gone she held my head as I puked into the toilet. She slept over twice. I shook and cried like a baby, not a grown man. She held my hand until I fell asleep at night.

Strange to have a woman in your bed — even an ex-sister-in-law — and feel nothing. I hadn't had an erection since discovering the affair. My darling beautiful wife had kicked me in the nuts from the grave.

The second time JP let himself in he found me on the porch. I had showered and shaved. The coffee I was drinking was half whiskey but at least I was functional.

He leaned against the iron railing. "Ça va?"

"Better."

"This has been a lot," he said and then coughed uncomfortably. No doubt it pained JP to say something sympathetic to anyone, especially me. He took out his cigarettes.

"I want to know what you've been up to," I said in English in case my voice was still shaky.

JP just lit his cigarette and blew smoke out over the gray morning street.

"I wanted to bring you in," he said shaking his head. "But it will be better if I just do this myself."

"Do what yourself?"

"This," he said, getting excited all of a sudden, waving his cigarette. "Justice for Liana!"

"What do you know?" I repeated, in French this time, losing my temper.

"Why do you care? This is over for you."

"Then why are you here, Jean-Paul? Why did you come find me again in the first place?"

"Because I thought maybe you'd still care. I thought you'd still want to murder the son of a bitch who did this to me. To us. There was a time you would've tore him limb from limb. That time is still now for me. But you," he practically spat. "You're lost."

"You don't think I tried to find out what happened? Why the hell do you think I stayed in this country?"

"I know why you stayed. I know what you are, who you work for."

"It's not a secret."

"Right, *the Embassy*. America's spy nest in Paris."

"Maybe you'd rather it be Soviet France?" I didn't give him time to respond with his usual tirade against the "great saviors" of France. "I just work there, JP. I'm not a spy."

He raised his brow. "It doesn't matter to me," he said.

"Tell me what you know. I can help."

I knew it was the wrong thing to say but I was still feeling banged up. My head hurt even with the whiskey.

"I don't want your fucking help!" he yelled, crushing the cigarette on the railing. He left the rest unsaid and headed for the door.

I didn't go after him.

Just sat at the little table where I used to have coffee with Liana, before walking her to the corner. There I'd held her thin body in my arms and kissed her goodbye. How could she have felt so solid, so warm? Now her ashes floated eternally on the brook behind Henri and Cosette's, the same place she asked me for courage.

I grabbed a pack of Lucky Strikes from my stash in the dresser and went back to Le Carré Rouge. Parisians always stick to the same café. I had one with Liana, where I never go. This place was more fitting. It was strictly bottom shelf. The regulars rolled their own cigarettes and there was always a table with a view of the traffic circle.

I knew what JP wanted. I remembered how I felt that first year. Living on hate, living for vengeance. When I wasn't drunk, I was bothering the police, calling in favors with the French services. I had been with the Sûreté when they questioned suspects. I skulked around Communist meetings, trying to pass myself off as an American comrade. But I was always suspect, and nobody opened up to me more than the usual propaganda line. I followed the men the Sûreté took in for questioning. Some for weeks at a time. Nothing out of the ordinary. No hatchet men. They were family men, working men, functionaries of the party. Rallies, meetings, strikes, canvassing, campaigning. Nothing violent. No one told any stories over drinks. They were dedicated to their cause but did nothing to make me think they had killed one of the opposition and my wife.

There had been no doubt about what I would do when I figured out who had killed Liana. Unintended bystander or not, they would pay with their own life. I had my Colt 1911 wrapped in an oiled cloth in the closet.

The fire that burned inside me never went out, but after that first year of disappointment and false leads, after fellow attachés reported to me that they figured it for the work of Russian agents on orders from the Kremlin, my blood lust began to seep away, like rain on a bridge drying in the sun.

Liana became one of the many senseless deaths. She might have been in a car accident, she might have choked or fallen down the stairs. Undignified. Unlucky. Like so many GIs, she had been in the wrong place at the wrong time.

And now — had JP found a string to pull?

Even if he had it probably didn't matter. I'd be shipped back to the States and debriefed any day now.

But maybe there was a way I could stay on, at least long enough to settle this.

I found JP at the same bar where he used to hang out when I was married to his daughter. He was sitting at a table playing *la belote* with friends or maybe enemies. I didn't know. They looked like mechanics. The bar was in the Eleventh, not far from Pere Lachaise, a working-class neighborhood. No professors here. Or immigrants. Natives only. Some Algerians had been beaten on the street only a week ago. Where were all those loyal colonized subjects of France supposed to go?

When he saw me he got up and went to the bar. He ordered Suze. The barman poured two cloudy glasses of the yellow liquor. Besides being one of the cheapest drinks, it was disgusting. I sometimes ordered it despite the taste of bitter orange peels.

"What do you want?"

"To kill someone," I said.

He looked into my eyes. His were red and puffy. "I don't believe you," he said, taking a drink. "But I'm going to need you. This time we finish it."

I took a drink and waited for him to tell me what he had found out.

"Philippe — that is his name — is a professor at the Sorbonne and also a communist. And, it seems, so was Liana."

I scoffed. "Don't you think I'd know that?"

"No," he replied bluntly. "I don't. As an American there are things you couldn't understand. The motives of a French woman are not the same as in your country. She couldn't sacrifice who she was for promises."

"She wasn't like that."

"But she was, wasn't she? You'll need to accept that. Accept she was not the perfect wife you thought she was. She was independent, she had a life she didn't share with you. Maybe she would have..." He stopped.

This was more than he'd said to me all at once the whole time I'd been his son-in-law.

He went back to his table and recovered his cigarette from the ashtray.

"Osval had a 15-year-old daughter. The police report has nothing about her."

"Police report?"

"I have a friend on the force. She'll be seventeen now, an adult. Maybe she knows something."

"And if she doesn't?" I asked. "Do we break her arm?"

JP smiled. "We'll see."

"Let me do it. Just stay in the car with your *tool kit*."

JP shrugged. "The downstairs neighbor in her building knows me anyways. I'll pick you up at noon. I've watched her. She never leaves the apartment before two. She's a dancer at Le Coq Gaulois, or maybe a *putain*."

I nodded and finished my drink without coughing.

"She should be alone, the mother leaves with the husband, or whatever he is, around ten. They part ways at the corner. I think she works for the post."

"And him?"

"I don't know. Wears a cheap suit and hangs around Les Halles market."

"Maybe it would be better to talk to the daughter at work."

"Who knows who'll be watching there. Better alone."

I left the bar and walked toward the metro. It was the kind of day I might have strolled through the flea market at Porte de Clignancourt, or the bookstalls along the Seine on the Left Bank. Maybe afterwards a drink with Liana on St. Germain or over the bridge to the Ile Saint Louis for a café.

Someone at the Embassy said they'd seen Picasso and Hemingway there. What it must have been like in Paris before the war.

When I got to the metro stairs I changed my mind and headed toward the Sorbonne. I hadn't been there in a long time. It was a lively part of Paris. Busy with students, those born just before the war.

I walked into the building where Liana had her classroom. I hadn't spent much time here. Occasionally I came in to meet her after class. It was always so bustling, so alive. Maybe it had too much, too much temptation. It occurred to me that I might find *him* here. The professor Liana found more exciting than me, who fit her academic mind better. Maybe she even loved him more. I pushed the thought away.

I found her old classroom and cracked the door. It was full of kids listening to a lecture. I went in and took a seat at the back.

It took me a few minutes to figure out the subject. Someone's textbook read *Abstract Expressionism*. Liana was part of this. Part of the new wave of art. The museums were full of Jackson Pollock and Helen Frankenthaler now. Liana painted and sculpted in experimental ways; the work resembled nothing of the subject. This was the future. I had encouraged her to turn tradition on its head, even if I preferred the old stuff. Giant paintings of battles, dogs with pheasants in their teeth and stags hung for dressing. I didn't understand the canvases of colorful blotches. It was lost on me. But Liana was passionate about it. The old stuff was overdone, belonged to the past, she'd say. Maybe that's what I was.

If she hadn't been killed, would we still be together? Or

would she have left me? How long would I have played the sap? Maybe she would have come back to me on her own. Maybe I would never have needed to know about Philippe.

I left the class. Her office was in another building, a half block away. I took the stairs to the fourth floor. They had given me the little name plaque with her things. There had also been a memorial for her at the school's graduation that year. All the students had stood, there was a chorus who sang La Mer. The professors all shook my hand afterwards. Including, I supposed, Philippe. I didn't remember. Maybe he'd had the decency not to. I doubted it, the fucking douche.

I knocked on the door. Her office was occupied by "Prof. Alois Courtemanche" now.

An older gentlemen answered in a tweed jacket. How stereotypical.

"I'm sorry to disrupt you."

"Come in, come in," he said. "You are Liana's husband."

"Yes."

"I remember seeing you now and then. I was so sorry," he said shaking my hand. "Someone with so much vitality, so much energy. And the way she understood art. What it could do, could mean."

I just looked down, nodding.

"She is missed here," he went on. "By everyone. It is an honor to have her office."

"Thank you. I feel like I didn't know this part of her very well."

"Please, sit down."

I sat and he pulled out a bottle of schnapps from his desk

drawer and took down two teacups from the shelf behind him. After pouring in a dash, he handed me one.

"This place, to me, was just where I lost her every day," I started. "I should have been... I wish I had been a bigger part of her art."

Alois watched me over his teacup, a strange look on his face. His eyes were blue and a little watery.

"But I think you were. I think you were a big part of her art. The school has a permanent collection you know. Can I show you something? Do you have time?"

"Yes, of course."

He finished his drink and smacked his lips. I set my cup on the desk and noticed a small bronze sculpture of a man sitting with a book. The sculpture had been there when this was Liana's desk.

"That sculpture..."

"Done by a professor who died during the war. It kind of lives here. This was also his office."

"What happened?"

"A dark chapter for France. The Gestapo came and took him one day. He was never seen again. I understand you were in the army?"

"The Third. The *occupying force* her father used to say."

The man chuckled. "Yes, we French are very patriotic. And for some, even when it was Vichy."

We took the stairs to a courtyard and crossed it to another gray stone building. In the basement he unlocked a room and flipped on the lights. It was a gallery of sorts. Objects under glass or freestanding and an array of paintings. I followed him to the far wall.

"Did Liana ever show this to you?"

"No," I said, mesmerized.

On a white table stood a glass tree, maybe three or four feet tall, on a wooden base with a drawer. I was sure it was meant to be a Black Walnut. They were Liana's favorite. Something to do with a place her parents had taken her as a child and the tree had become her solace.

There were two trunks at the base that twisted into one. The branches were hollow, with the tips of each branch open, like the end of a straw. The glass reflected different colors, muted but noticeable, hints of green, rust, light blue and beige. They felt familiar somehow.

Alois pulled out the drawer. Inside was a flat reel-to-reel recorder. He pressed a button and the tapes turned. Liana's voice came out of the speakers. At first I thought she may have been reading a book. But the sentences didn't make sense. It was a jumble of words.

"What is she reading?" I asked.

Alois just shook his head slightly.

I recognized the words somehow. The intonation of her voice. She wasn't reading random words. They came from somewhere else, someplace meaningful to her.

He pushed the drawer in and the words became a hum, echoes, musical almost, escaping through the branches.

Alois said nothing but looked at the piece with me another minute. I was awestruck.

"I wanted you to see it," he said, opening the drawer and turning off the tape.

I followed him out and he locked the door.

"Thank you," I said. "I'm really at a loss for words."

"Come back anytime," he said, shaking my hand.

I had the feeling he didn't want to talk anymore. Something had changed and he was uncomfortable now.

At the front steps he gave me another tight-lipped smile and walked away.

What didn't he want to say? What, I wondered, was he doing during the war? Probably teaching here. Life went on in Paris despite shortages and hardships.

At the corner of the building, I turned and walked deeper into campus. I used to feel out of place here. It was such a different world. Everyone was young and hopelessly pessimistic.

Now I felt like everyone's father. Not jealous anymore. They didn't have Liana. None of us did. Instead, I could look at them for what they were. Hadn't I brought the light back into the world for them? That's what they told us anyways. Our sacrifice was for their generation. And here they were.

I sat down on a bench and watched the students. I smoked a cigarette and pictured Liana's glass sculpture and the sound it made. What did it mean? Why had she never shown me?

I finished the cigarette but didn't get up. To move from this spot was to rejoin the world outside. To get back to the black tunnel leading... where?

Chapter Two

JP WAS EARLY. THE PASSENGER DOOR to his work van scraped as I pulled it closed. He stuck it in gear and it whined forward. I knew during the war he'd had a truck that ran on steam.

"The mother, Nadine," JP said as we picked up speed down rue Rivoli, "told the police she was glad Osval was dead. That he was a cheating bastard, a lousy father, and so on. I talked to the lady downstairs a week ago. She obviously detests Nadine, said there was a man living in the apartment a week after Osval's death. His supposed brother."

"You don't think he was just helping out," I suggested.

"Not from the look she gave. This brother was not interviewed either." JP pulled a wallet from his jacket pocket and handed it to me.

A badge and Sûreté ID card. They looked fake to me but would probably fool a teenager.

"See if she remembers anyone coming around, making threats. Ask her about Osval's *brother*."

I nodded, stuffed the wallet in my pocket and tried my Parisian accent on JP. "Je suis avec la Sûreté."

"It's not good, but passable," he said. "There are other

things you should know." JP slowed for traffic and looked at me. "Things Philippe said."

I showed nothing, but felt a hot flush, and my heart beat faster. What else didn't I know?

"I went to the Sorbonne to talk to him."

"I'm sure he was happy to see you," I said.

JP smiled. "Liana was attending communist meetings. Not as an official member, maybe out of deference to your position, but she was a regular. Philippe also said he tried picking her up off the sidewalk. The police report had both of them walking east. But Osval was heading west, coming toward her. Maybe it means nothing. I don't know. He said they were laying about two meters apart."

Two meters. That seemed far enough to avoid shooting her.

"And he said the car was speeding around the corner of rue d'Ulm. She would not have been facing them. She would not have seen them until they had turned. And if they blacked out the license plate, she would know nothing."

They had killed her just because. A precaution.

JP sped us around a traffic circle and turned. We were in the eighteenth arrondissement. A neighborhood being mixed with Moroccans and Vietnamese. After a block he pulled the van over.

"Philippe also said he was not expecting Liana that day. She had broken the affair off but wanted to talk about working together. He admitted he had been making things difficult for her at school."

Sweat dampened my brow. It was too much to make sense of.

JP pointed to the building across the street.

"It's number ten."

I pushed my hair back and tried to focus. I remembered how I sometimes imitated a Parisian snob to make Liana laugh.

"I need a moustache," I said.

JP chuckled. "You'll be alright. Good luck, I'll keep an eye." He patted the tool kit sitting between us.

I got out of the car. The sun was out now, and it promised a clear day. I crossed the street into shadow and found the buzzer.

An old woman answered the door.

"Police, Madame. I need to speak to," I checked a little notebook I had in my coat pocket. "Zelie Delage."

"Second floor," she said, pointing up the stairs.

"Merci."

I went up to the second landing and knocked on the door. A woman in a bathrobe with a severe look on her face peered out. Her hair was wrapped in a scarf.

"Madame Delage?" I said with a sudden lump in my throat.

"Yes, what do you want?"

"You have a daughter? Zelie?"

She opened the door wider. A cigarette I hadn't seen was between the fingers of her right hand.

I took out my ID. Her eye flicked upward. Did she know it was a fake? Maybe she'd seen many of these before.

"What has the little whore done now?"

"It is a complaint she may be able to help us with, nothing serious."

"Wait here."

From the kitchen a shirtless man leaned against the fridge

where he could get a look at me. He was paunchy but solid looking. His neck was abnormally thick. He rubbed his unshaven face and then moved off.

The girl came into the room, followed by her mother, and stood in front of me with hand on hip. I rocked back on my heels a bit at the sight of her. Taller than her mother, thin as a waif, with legs that made her skirt seem very short. She had long blonde hair and blue eyes that drilled right through my head. I tried to remember she was only 17.

"We need privacy," I said.

"We can talk in my room. But I've done nothing wrong." She brushed her mother aside and I followed her down a short hall. She closed the door behind us and sat on the bed.

Her room was barren like a prison cell. I imagined she felt like a caged lion.

She lifted her eyebrows. "They know you are not the police," she whispered very matter-of-factly. "As soon as you leave they will ask me what you wanted."

"Merde," I said under my breath. A soft creak came from the hallway.

"I just need to ask you a few questions," I said loudly, maybe overdoing it. "About your boss, Romain, the owner of Le Coq Gaulois."

"Hardly know him," she said. Then whispered, "What do you really want?"

I wanted to be tactful but had no time. "Your father, Osval," I whispered. "I need to ask you about his death."

"Romain's a sweetheart, everyone loves him," she said in her natural voice. "But I don't know anything about his business."

"What about the people he meets regularly with, do you know them?"

She looked at me for a long moment. Did I look like someone she could trust? I had no idea.

"Find me at work tonight," she whispered. "It will cost you a bottle of champagne, but we can talk privately."

I nodded.

"No," she said. "I know no one."

"Merci, pour le renseignement, mademoiselle."

She got up and walked slowly to the door. Did she want me to see her from behind? She would be an unbelievable beauty someday. Maybe Chanel would discover her and put her on the catwalk. More likely, if she was a dancer at Le Coq, she'd end up with a *vieux protecteur*.

She did not see me out. I walked down the hallway where the man, now dressed, stood by the door. The woman was nowhere to be seen.

"Good day," I said, nodding to him. He looked at me with the blank eyes of a shark and said nothing.

I walked past JP's Citroen H Van parked on the other side of the street and took a left at the next block. I knew he'd figure it out. He picked me up on Marcadet.

"Christ! The mother was there and so was the brother. I've seen GIs with the same look he had. He's dangerous."

"He was watching you walk down the sidewalk from the window. Not a man you want to cross."

I had a feeling we'd be crossing a lot of people soon.

"You think she knows something?" JP probed.

"Maybe," I shrugged. "She said to meet her later at work."

"So she can get some money out of you."

I ignored him. "I didn't get the feeling they were a very happy family."

"Where should I take you?"

"My place. I'll let you know what I find out tomorrow."

"Should I be there?"

"I don't think so, I'll be alright."

JP pulled up at the corner of Pont Neuf and I got out.

"Watch out for her," he said. "She's a siren."

I walked to my door and wondered where JP was going. To fix a toilet somewhere? From plotting murder to fixing leaky sinks.

My apartment was dark and quiet. It had been for two years. Why hadn't I gotten a dog? Where the hell did Liana's cat go? Had she been run over? Or had the fat devil sensed Liana was not coming back and left?

I hardly noticed the pile of boxes in the bedroom closet anymore. I knew they were there: sketchbooks, drawings, school work. All the stuff from her office. I had never opened them, just picked them up. I didn't think I was meant to. They were Liana's private record of her life apart from mine.

And now? Would I find love notes between them? Did she scribble her feelings in the margins of books? The thought froze me. What did it matter anymore? I couldn't go on thinking I knew everything about her. Maybe they would tell me why. Why she was unhappy with me.

Fuck it.

I closed the closet door and lay on the bed. I knew I would cry again. I was cracked. I would sit on this bed and cry for the rest of my life.

My head ached when I finally pushed myself up off the bed. Outside, day had faded to night. I felt disjointed.

I went into the bathroom and ran a hot shower. I looked in the mirror, my eyes were puffy. I noticed a crease between my brows and little bumps under my eyes I didn't recall a year ago. My hair was still dark, but receding, and there was a shimmer of silver in my sideburns. I was getting old. Somehow, I'd never noticed it when Liana was alive.

It occurred to me I hadn't tried to pick up a woman since before the war. But maybe I should try. Or was that part of my life over?

I sensed the impossible truth. I was waiting for Liana.

I shaved, showered and put on the suit I wore to informal Embassy parties. It was gray with pin stripes. Dark ties were what people wore now in Paris. I put on a gray one with blue stripes. I needed to look like a high-roller at a place like this.

Next to my suit on the rack was my uniform. I saw U.S. servicemen walking around now and then. Maybe that would give me some anonymity at Le Coq. An officer attached to some NATO base on R & R.

Officially I'd been demobbed in '46, the same year Liana and I were married. Unofficially Eisenhower was still my commanding officer. I slapped my palm against my gut. My uniform was probably two sizes too small now. All that damn French bread and cheese. I went with the suit.

Outside, it was cooler than I expected. I hailed a cab once I walked across Pont Neuf. The cabby was black and spoke with an American accent.

"Stay on after the war?" I asked.

"Oh, I went home," he answered spiritedly. "That's how come I'm back again."

We both laughed. It was a screwed-up world.

What would it be like for me back in the States? I didn't have a good feeling.

I got off at Clichy in Montmartre and walked uphill the rest of the way. The streets were busy with young people out for a good time. The workday was over — if they had a job. France was in the midst of another long economic slowdown. The communists and socialists were tearing each other apart, and sometimes the rhetoric turned violent in the streets. Meanwhile everything stood still. I walked past a shell game being played on the sidewalk. A thin Asian woman, Vietnamese probably, floated out from the shadow of a doorway and tried to slide her arm through mine. Everyone was coming to France now.

"Not tonight," I said.

She faded back.

Le Coq Gaulois was on the corner with a grand façade of a doorway. Two black men in suits stood at the entrance. I wasn't riff raff tonight. They let me in with a nod.

The entrance led to a long stairway down. At the bottom was a large open space, a maze of tables and a dozen or so oval stages, most with women dancing. The closest shimmered in sequins and bare skin. Others seemed to sparkle despite having nothing on but belts or top hats or high heels.

The clientele was *chic*. I had chosen the right outfit. I walked to the bar in the back of the room and looked around for Zelie. She was not on any of the stages. No one was on the main stage. Cigarette girls slipped through the tables. And then I noticed a kind of uniform. Women sitting at tables with the most petit dresses. Long legs exposed from the upper thigh to heels below. Some wore sparkling chokers around their neck. All of them young. All of them beautiful. No doubt Zelie belonged to this army.

The barman came over and I ordered a Pernod. It was awful stuff, but it would keep me sharp. I looked over the patrons, mostly men, sitting at the tables, entranced by the entertainment. A boisterous lot near the stage drew my attention. One of the dancers had draped her arms around a man from behind. He caressed them with franc notes fanned out like feathers in his hands. I recognized his fat face; it was the man I'd seen with Alix. When my drink arrived, I asked the bartender who he was.

"Nobody you'd want to know, monsieur."

I held his wrist. "Pretend I do."

He leaned closer. "Ludo Orban."

The great mobster of Paris. I nodded my thanks.

"Buy a lady a drink?"

I almost didn't recognize her with the make-up, deep red lipstick, and hair in a tight bun over her head. She stood four inches taller in heels.

She put her hand firmly on my cock and then ran it up my chest and down my arm where it stayed. I felt a tingling sensation everywhere her hand had traveled, and it was a sensation I hadn't felt in a long time.

"What does the lady want?" I asked, clearing my throat.

"Pierre," she called over the bar.

The barman returned.

"L'homme veut une bouteille de champagne."

He raised his eyebrows slightly at me and I nodded in return.

"Four thousand francs."

I pulled the bills from my wallet. A waiter in a white

jacket collected the bottle and two glasses onto a tray and led us along the back wall of the bar. Zelie held my arm as we crossed under an archway into a dark room, couches and low tables partially obscured by a maze of velvet curtains. He set the tray down at a table and popped the cork.

I tipped him and he left after pouring two fizzing glasses.

"It is expected that you will tip me too."

"That depends," I said.

She smiled and her hand found its way to the front of my slacks again.

"Not on that."

She pulled me down to the couch and then reached for a champagne flute.

"Do they know how young you are?" I asked.

"Why? Are you really the police?"

"No, I'm just a concerned citizen."

"There are younger girls," she said with a shrug. "I let men drool down my neck so I can get out of that hell hole you found me in. Is that so bad?" She didn't wait for an answer. "Nothing else, other than being a prostitute, could make me enough. There's a housing shortage you know."

"Yes, I know."

"But for you, I might give you something special." I felt her hand on my leg.

I held it where it was on my thigh. "I just need information."

"So you said. But you paid for the champagne, you might as well *drink* it."

After a pregnant pause she leaned forward and brought a glass back for me. I hadn't had champagne since my anniversary. I brought it to my lips. It was brut, not the cheap crap I thought it might be. Her hand returned to my inner thigh and I didn't stop it moving to my hard-on. She finished the rest of her champagne and swished it around her mouth and then put her head on my shoulder. I knew what was coming if I let it. All I had to do was do nothing. I rested my cheek against her soft hair and for just a moment enjoyed the sensation of her inquisitive fingers.

She stretched up to kiss my ear and I snapped back to earth, grabbed her hand and moved it off me. She slid over on the couch and gave me a venomous look.

"Like I said, I'm just here for information."

"Why the hell should I tell you anything?"

I knew I should lie; I didn't know her and she could be dangerous. But I ignored the caution.

"I'm trying to find your father's killer."

"Why? He was an asshole. And he wasn't my father."

She moved a bit closer again. "My real father was killed during the invasion. I was three."

"I'm sorry."

I took her hand and held it. The anger ran away from her face.

She shrugged. "When I was ten Osval moved in. He was a sadist. He spanked me so hard I couldn't sit down at school. He almost killed my mother. After him I got my 'Uncle' Yannick. Until maybe a year ago he'd come into my room at night. I didn't know what he was doing. I would just hear him breathing. I pretended to be asleep."

"He didn't touch you?"

She shook her head and shuddered a little. "I think he masturbated. Maybe my mother caught on. Now he just looks at me, like he's biding his time. It makes me go cold."

I didn't know what to say. I finished my drink.

"Whoever killed Osval also murdered my wife," I confessed. "She just happened to be there on the sidewalk."

"I know about her. What was she doing with Osval?"

"They weren't together."

Zelie was silent a few moments and toyed with her rings.

"Your *Uncle* Yannick, does he have a job?" I asked.

"I think he collects. You know, from people who make bets."

That explained why he hung around Les Halles.

"And his politics?" I pressed.

"I've seen flyers for PNU in the kitchen."

PNU, or *le Parti de l'Unité Nationale,* was one of the new right-wing parties.

"My mother too. She always goes to their stupid meetings." Zelie turned to me and moved her hand out from mine. "Do you really think you can find who did this?"

"I don't know. But anything you know might help. Anything you can tell me about Osval."

"Other than being a piece of shit."

I smiled. "Yes, other than that."

She reached for the champagne and filled her glass.

"You don't mind, do you? I like the bubbles."

"I'll give you a thousand francs too."

"Keep your money, I don't want it."

"Then let me put you up for a while. Until you've saved enough." I said it before I'd even thought.

She looked at me sideways. "Pour de vrai?"

I nodded. "You'll just have to pretend to be my niece."

She narrowed her brow. "The kind of nieces rich men have?"

I shook my head. "Like a sweet, innocent, well-behaved niece. And nobody can know where you're staying. And…" I looked at her, feeling embarrassed. "And no men."

"Uncle! What do you think I am?"

She was very cheery now and poured the rest of the champagne into our glasses. "A toast. To my new home."

"Temporary new home," I corrected.

"Of course, *Uncle*," she said winking.

We clinked glasses.

She drank hers down in one gulp.

"There's only one thing I can think of that might help you. It may be nothing."

"What?"

"I took the wrong bus from school once. It went way out of the way, but I knew it would get me close enough to home if I just stayed on it. Then I saw him on the sidewalk, Osval. I got off at the corner and caught up with him. I thought I might catch him meeting some woman. I thought, I'll tell Mother and let her crucify him. But he went into a bar. If I went in, he'd see me. I stood against the wall and peeked through the window. It was the afternoon; the place was mostly empty. Osval went up to the counter and the bartender kissed him. On the lips. I went back to the bus stop. I never told Mother. I didn't know what it meant."

"Do you remember the bar?"

"It was three years ago," she protested. "But I think I could find it. I would remember the stop if we took the same bus."

"When can we meet? Tomorrow? Are you okay going home tonight?"

"Yes, and yes. But if you give the bartender 2,000 francs we can leave now."

"Let's go then."

She took the bottle and tipped the last stream of champagne into her mouth. Then led me out through the archway and to the bar. Pierre took the money and told me to have a good night. Zelie disappeared for her coat and purse and then held my arm as we climbed the stairs.

Outside we turned left toward Clichy. The streets were still busy, the city of lights living up to its reputation. Zelie's painted face seemed only slightly out of place outside the club. She must have noticed my glance.

"I look like a circus performer, don't I?"

"Un peu."

She pulled me into a café. "Wait here."

I stood near the door. The café had just a few gray-haired patrons. I looked out the open doorway and watched the couples go by. And what about me? Forty years old. I didn't look like these kids anymore, but I didn't belong in this café either. I still didn't *feel* old.

I heard Zelie clicking her way back to me when I saw someone stop at the corner across the street. I could tell it was a man from the way he lit his cigarette.

Zelie was standing next to me now, framed in the doorway for anyone to see.

"Ready?" she asked.

"Across the street," I said.

The man quickly turned the corner and disappeared.

"Yannick?" she whispered.

"Maybe."

"It was him." She pulled me into the street. "Does this change anything?"

"No," I said. "Let's catch that bus."

"We need to…" She looked around, disoriented. Yannick had unnerved her. It unnerved me. I didn't know what to make of it. Was he just watching out for Zelie? Or was there more to it?

"Is he protective of you?"

"Jealous more like. But I didn't think he was keeping tabs on me." She crossed the street. "We have to go the way he did."

I nodded. He was either gone for the night or we'd come across him again. I felt for the Colt under my right armpit.

Clichy ran upward toward Place de Stalingrad. I caught myself looking in doorways and the windows of bars and cafés but Yannick was gone.

"The bus went down Boulevard de Rochechouart, at the top of the hill," Zelie said.

I was more out of breath than I should have been. I needed to get back into shape. Stop smoking too. We stood at the bus stop with an ancient black woman and a couple of teens who should have been home.

"Did you love her, your wife?" Zelie asked, uncertainty in her tone.

"Yes. I did."

"And still? You still do?"

I looked down at the gum-stained sidewalk. "I still do."

"I've never been in love," she said.

"You're young. There's time."

"No, there's not. I'll just have men who want me. They won't let me love them. Then I'll get old, and it will be over for me. Maybe when I'm…" She tilted her head toward the old woman on the bench. "I'll find someone to love. Right before I punch out."

I laughed a little, to let her know this was nonsense. But I wasn't sure it was. If she stayed at Le Coq, blossoming more and more, she would be in demand by men looking for arm candy, for validation of their manhood. But they wouldn't let it go too far. She could very well end up alone. Like me.

Zelie smiled, to say I shouldn't worry about her even though she was right.

"Your life is what you make it," I said. The bus punctuated my words of wisdom by coming up the hill. Zelie helped the lady up from the bench.

Even at this hour the trip seemed to take forever. Zelie used my shoulder as a head rest and the warmth of her was bringing back all kinds of unwelcome feelings.

"Are you sure this is right?" I asked.

"Yes, eventually it gets back up to Marcadet. Look at the map."

At the front of the bus, over the driver, there was a crooked map. I couldn't read it from here but could see the bump where it must have gone up toward Zelie's place.

She looked out the window. After another stop, she got up, stepped over me, and crossed the aisle.

"We're getting close I think. It was daytime, but I remember those stalls. If there's a bookstore with a red sign. Look on that side just in case."

After another block and a half Zelie bolted up and grabbed my arm. "This is it!"

We moved to the front of the bus and the driver pulled over.

Zelie was excited now and pulled me down the street.

"The bar is on the corner."

I held her back and she tugged against me. This was a

game to her. I didn't let go and she stopped pulling. She leaned backwards into me.

"Don't you want to go in?"

"Just wait a second."

I could feel the nervous energy pulsing through her.

"Zelie, take some deep breaths. Will you recognize him?"

She tilted her head. "I think so."

"I need you to know so."

She took two deep breaths and put her head back against my shoulder. She started to relax. "I will."

"Good."

I took her by the hand and walked the few feet to the door and pulled it open. The place was nearly pitch black. The street under the lamp posts was like broad daylight in comparison. We stood just inside the door until my eyes adjusted. It was not busy, a few patrons at the bar and a couple tables occupied against the opposite wall. It was all men, but that was not unusual in Paris. I kept Zelie's warm hand in mine and stepped up to the bar. It seemed we were getting more attention from the barflies than I would have expected. Or was it just her?

The man who came over to us was drying a glass with a rag. In school he would have been teased as a pretty boy. In his late 20s, floppy hair cut straight across his forehead.

"Deux Pernod s'il vous plaît," I said.

Zelie made a "blech" sound. "Deux Chambord," she instructed.

He looked at Zelie for an extra second and turned around. I glanced over but she shook her head.

"He was shorter, with slicked graying hair," she whispered.

The four men at the bar looked working class. Smoking cigarettes, the two closest appraised us with smirks. We sat on the tall wood stools and waited for our drinks. I probably looked like a john who'd brought his young hooker to the wrong bar. The two men in the corner lost interest in us and started talking to each other.

"What will we do?" Zelie asked.

I lifted an eyebrow at her. Fucked if I knew.

Our drinks came and I fished out some francs from my pocket.

"I was hoping to see the bartender I met last time," I said casually.

He shrugged. "There is only the owner. He'll be in later tonight."

"Shorter than you? Graying hair."

He nodded, furrowing his brow. Whatever perplexed him he didn't share it. He swept the coins over his side and walked away.

"This might be a long night," I said.

"It's okay. I want to do this."

She was a decent girl, I thought. She didn't care who killed Osval. And I didn't think she wanted money or to be rewarded. She was helping me just to get some justice.

The two at the far end were looking at us again. Maybe we should be better at playing our part. I took some coins out of my pocket and stepped to the jukebox. I played a popular French song, "La Vie en rose," and it came on much louder than I expected. Edith Piaf's shrill voice filled the room.

Zelie got the idea and met me on the floor. She wrapped her arms around me, and everyone watched us as we swayed to the music. She pulled away slightly and moved smoothly. I was a shit dancer, and just tried not to trip her up. She made it seem easy, moving her hips more than her feet. Maybe it was to avoid having her toes crushed. The next song was faster, and she playfully swung our arms and twisted her waist. Then, keeping her hands on me, she danced around me and I had no problem playing the fool for my young *putain*.

We danced and drank for another hour. I had started to sweat. Two men who had been sitting at a table also started to dance. The bar was filling up now. I finally pulled Zelie back to our stools at the bar.

"Let's get some fresh air," she said.

I followed her out. It was cool and quiet on the street. I put two cigarettes to my lips and lit them. She took one and inhaled deeply, then lifting her head like a wolf, expelled a plume of aromatic smoke.

"I like you, Eli," she said, smiling.

"I like you too, Zelie."

She took another drag and gave me a serious look. "Have you had anyone, any girlfriends since…"

I shook my head. "She was the only one," *for me*, I didn't quite finish.

"Sounds kind of lonely."

"Maybe," I said.

"Maybe you're just scared."

I shrugged. "Maybe I am."

Zelie stubbed out her cigarette and then her eyes grew big, and she tugged my arm. I looked over my shoulder as a man reached for the door.

I moved backward a step and blocked the door with my foot.

"Pardon," he snapped.

"I'm sorry, Monsieur, but I wonder if we could talk a minute."

"Who the fuck are you?" he said with growing hostility. He looked me over and then seemed to relax a bit. I was too big to tangle with. Zelie took the Lucky Strikes from my shirt pocket and held them out to him.

"I'm Zelie."

"Francois," he offered, accepting the cigarette.

I pulled out my matches and gave him a light.

"I'm trying to find out who killed my Papa," Zelie said convincingly. "We need your help."

"Moi? Are you serious?"

"Yes, you knew him," Zelie said, choking up. "Osval Delage."

The man loosened his collar and took a frustrated drag off the cigarette.

"I never heard of him," he finally said.

"The thing is," Zelie said, "I know you did."

Francois glared at Zelie and then at me. "And you're who? Her bodyguard?"

"It's complicated," I smiled. "I'm just helping her find the truth."

"If you're who you say you are, who's your mother? Where do you live? What did your father smoke?"

"My mother is Nadine, we live on rue Lamarck, and all my life Papa smoked Gitanes."

"You look nothing like him," he said, defeated, stamping out the half-smoked cigarette.

"I take after my mother."

"I never met her," he said under his breath. "I really don't know anything about Osval. We were... friends. But I can't help you. I hardly knew him."

"Maybe it's a little thing. Something that doesn't seem important," I coaxed.

"Do you have another cigarette?"

I held out the pack.

He used his own lighter and drew smoke eagerly now. "I didn't even know what had happened until I read it in the paper. The things they said about him. Like it was all about somebody else. A member of the PNU? A known collaborator? It seemed impossible."

Zelie looked at me with an expression of incredulity. I just squinted at her.

"We usually met here, but a few times we went out, to the park, or club that catered to our crowd."

"Did anything out of the ordinary happen?"

"It was a happy time for me. I felt..." He was embarrassed now. He brought the cigarette to his lips.

"It's okay. We are not here to judge you," Zelie said.

"Well, it's all shit anyways. Only once that I can think of, in the park, Osval suddenly left me, like he didn't even know who I was. I nearly..."

A furrow creased his forehead. He was looking across the street.

"I have to go," he said, stubbing out his cigarette. "Sorry I can't be more help."

With that he got by me and went in the bar.

I looked across the street but only saw the backside of someone taking the corner.

I took Zelie's hand and we headed back to the bus stop.

"Can you pay for a cab?"

"Yes," I said.

"I just want to get home. To your home."

I looked at her sideways. She seemed a little sick.

I opened my front door and led Zelie up to the second floor and unlocked my apartment door. Other than my sister-in-law, Zelie was the only woman I'd brought home since Liana died. I hadn't thought about what it might look like to someone other than myself. It was a mess. I thought to clean the bathroom and do the dishes quickly.

"Sorry," I said.

"It's not like you were expecting company."

"No," I said. "Your room is next to mine. The bed is made, nobody's used it."

I walked her down the hall and opened the door. I'd kept some of Liana's things there. In the closet she would find a few dresses, shoes, hats. I couldn't get rid of them. I couldn't let go.

"It's perfect," she said, sitting on the bed. "Thank you."

"Of course," I said. "We need to figure out why Yannick was following you before you can go back there."

"Do you think it could have something to do with this?"

"Doubtful," I replied. "Was Osval really his brother?"

"He never came to the house before Osval died. But they were both in the PNU. They might have known each other."

"Was there anyone Osval was very close to? Someone who used to come over or you saw him with?"

"There was someone. I used to think he was Osval's boss."

"Why?"

45

"Just from the way he spoke to him, like he was in charge. That Osval had to do what he wanted."

"Anything else? Any enemies he cursed about?"

"Just communists. Probably because they weren't assholes like himself."

I smirked.

"You should smile more," she said.

I patted her leg and got up. "Let's get some sleep."

She laid back and put her head on the pillow. "Goodnight."

"Goodnight, Zelie."

I was tired enough to go to bed but went into the kitchen instead. There was a new whiskey bottle on the table and a half loaf of bread. JP must have brought the whiskey the last time he came over. I got some ice from the freezer, one of the few in Paris, and poured a short tumbler. Threlfall's. From Ireland. Just like JP to buy whiskey from anyone but the Brits and Yanks. I brought my drink and buttered bread to the couch in the living room.

Did Yannick mean Zelie harm? Or me? Why was he following us? Was he the shadow that turned when Francois zipped up? I wondered if there was any way to get Zelie out of this. She didn't need to be involved.

I would have to run this all by JP. I swirled the ice around in my glass and finished the whiskey. It was too sweet for my taste. But not bad. I heard the door open down the hall and then Zelie came out into the room wearing only her pink panties and bra.

She had a hard little body, but soft where it should be.

"I was wondering if you had an extra toothbrush?"

"No, but I have toothpaste. Use your finger. Tomorrow we'll get you a proper kit."

"I'll need to go to my mother's. We can go after they both leave so there's no drama."

"Tomorrow then."

She gave me a wave, turned and sauntered down the hallway. "Goodn-i-g-h-t."

"Goodnight," I said feeling like a deflated balloon.

Her perfume, something tropical, lingered in the room.

I dropped more ice into my glass and sloshed in some whiskey. After taking a slug I stomped into my bedroom and started hauling boxes into the living room. They were light for the most part and I took two at a time. After a few minutes I had a dozen boxes piled in front of the couch. It took me the length of another drink to open the first box. When I did, I toppled the contents out onto the coffee table. Sketchbooks, pens, pencils, erasers, brushes, a set of little keys, rubber bands, a pencil sharpener, some loose papers, memos, a small thin box, announcements for art shows and staff meetings.

I opened the small box and found a reel-to-reel tape inside. The label read "Tree Project." It must have been the backup tape or maybe an earlier draft for her glass sculpture. I imagined most of this stuff in the top drawer of her desk. I flipped through the sketchbooks. I recognized some drawings that became sculptures and some she must have abandoned as only ideas. The Politics section of a newspaper from 1951. Fliers, mostly for art shows we sometimes went to together. A few were for political rallies, none of them communist. But one orange flier for a PNU rally. I put the box to the lip of the table and used my arm to push everything back in. Everything but the tape.

The next box was the heaviest. Notebooks, sketchbooks, a few art books and student essays held together with clasps.

I took a good strong drink before flipping through the notebooks. But I found nothing that wasn't school related. Class notes, lesson plans, essays on modern art that she was either working on or had published in journals. I looked across at the barrister bookcase where some of them sat. She didn't think much of them. Just part of her job. But I was so proud that she was a published writer. Tucked into one of them, I couldn't remember which, was a letter from Sartre making a positive comment about her essay on classism in art.

I wasn't looking for clues to her affair. And I doubted there'd be anything to help me understand why she wanted to be a communist. I didn't know what I hoped to find. Some kind of sense of her again? To see her handwriting? Read her thoughts? No, I didn't think so. I just needed to process them. The whiskey was keeping me from articulating what my purpose was.

But this was *her*. An artist. A professional. This wasn't the part that belonged to me. This was the part that was only Liana's. The part I didn't really know. Had she wanted it that way? Or did I not want to know? Maybe I should have tried harder to understand this side of her.

But wasn't it okay if she had something that was just hers? I never admitted to being a part-time spy. Was that wrong? And I couldn't very well explain America's clandestine plan for having a covert army in France in case Russian tanks rolled down the Champs Elysees. That was literally top-secret information.

So that was my bit and making art was hers. But maybe she needed someone who *could* understand that about her. Maybe she wanted to know *everything* about me and for me to know everything about her. My dishonesty was real even if I didn't think of it that way. Maybe it felt good to be with someone like Philippe who understood her artist side. Or at least pretended too.

Maybe I really should break that asshole's legs.

I hurled a sketchbook across the room and knocked a photograph off the wall. Maybe I should burn them. What did I owe this faithless bitch?

The room was moving in a slow circle. I managed to get up and pour more whiskey into my glass. I didn't bother with the ice. There were still eight more boxes.

Chapter Three

AFTER MY MORNING CIGARETTE ON THE PORCH, I got a
phone call from Alois Courtemanch, the old professor at the
Sorbonne. He wanted me to come by his office again at 1:00.
After taking Zelie to collect some things at her mother's I
handed her the spare key and headed off to the university.

"I'm sorry I didn't show this to you," he said. "It was
in the top drawer." He handed me a photograph. "Under a
false bottom."

He pulled out the drawer to demonstrate.

The photo was a black and white candid of a handsome
young man, his hair caught in the wind. He was coming out
a door and looking up the street. I guessed he wasn't aware
of being photographed.

"The professor taken away by the Gestapo. Gael Favret."

"Were they close, Liana and Gael?"

"It wasn't unusual for a professor to have a favorite student," he answered.

I wondered if there was more to it.

"Was Gael in the Resistance?"

Alois shook his head. "Those years we all minded our
own business. Nobody wanted to know too much about
what other people did. But why else would they take him?"

I studied the picture. He looked like a man carrying all the problems of the world on his shoulders.

"I've never shown this to anyone," he continued, a pained look on his face. "I thought to destroy it many times because of what it might imply. But we both know Liana could never have had anything to do with Gael's death at the hands of the Gestapo. There were many Frenchmen who traded in human lives at that time, but Liana was certainly not one of them."

I agreed readily, but it didn't explain why she had this photo hidden in her desk.

"You did the right thing," I said. "Better we keep this between us."

"It's yours now. It was always yours. I apologize again for keeping it from you."

I could tell he was relieved to be rid of it.

"It's okay," I said, looking down again at the photo and feeling the sudden weight of Gael's death in my hands.

"Don't be too hard on yourself, Eli. The loss of someone like Liana..."

I tucked the photograph in my jacket pocket and nodded. "Thanks, Professor, thanks for everything."

He waved it off. "I hope you'll let me know what this was all about."

"Sure I will," I said, still not wanting to get up and leave. "I'll let you know."

He nodded and took the bottle of schnapps from his desk drawer.

Back at my apartment I poured myself a short whiskey over ice and took another look at the photo.

Had Liana taken it? Had *he* given it to her? The writing on the back was in French, but not Liana's hand. It said "Gael Favret / 36 rue St. Augustin / Oct. 3, '42." Was the photo meant to be part of a file?

I gulped down the whiskey. I checked my pockets for cigarettes but came up empty. I thought to get a pack from the drawer but sucked on the slivers of ice instead. Why had Liana kept the photo hidden?

Four whiskies later, long after I'd given up on divining an answer, I heard a key in the door. It was late, the radio that had been playing jazz had signed off.

I expected Zelie, tired after a night of selling champagne to slobbering men. But it was Alix who came in. I felt the familiar little catch in my chest when I saw her. It was that hint of Liana. It evaporated when my brain caught up with my heart.

She didn't look like she'd been out on the town as usual. She was dressed in a plain navy skirt and blouse, her heels were low. She saw me on the couch and closed the door.

"I thought you might be up."

"And if I hadn't been?"

"I'd have stopped in tomorrow," she said.

"Sounds important."

"It's not. I wanted to check on you. It wasn't long ago you needed me to hold your hand to fall asleep."

"That was kind of you, Alix."

She sat down next to me.

"I'm done in," she said.

"You don't look it. Were you out tonight?"

"No, I played cards with Papa. He's not well."

"What do you mean?"

"He's just so angry all the time, he's bursting. The old goat's going to have a heart attack."

"The bit's between his teeth."

"And you keep it there," she accused.

"He wants my help."

She got back up and moved toward the kitchen. "Mind if I pour myself a glass?"

"Help yourself," I said. I was too drunk to do it for her.

"Wouldn't it be best if we all just moved on?" she said, coming back into the room. "What's to be gained by digging up the past?"

I wasn't surprised by Alix's line of thinking. The past for her included getting her head shorn after liberation, and worse. I always thought the reason Liana wasn't close to her sister was because she had dated German officers during the occupation. Was there some other reason? What else did Alix want to leave behind?

She sat down next to me again.

"Some things can't be buried, not yet anyway," I said. "Don't you want someone to pay?"

"You mean other than all of us? All of us who've paid every day for what happened to my sister? You, my family, torn apart."

Her eyes teared up and she put her head on my shoulder.

"My mother couldn't take it, Papa's obsession. All he thinks about is getting revenge."

I didn't know what to say.

"You of all people must know she wouldn't want it. She hated violence. Hated all the death of the war. She'd want you to let it go."

I put my arm around her, but the tears kept coming.

"I didn't know you felt this way," I said.

She leaned back and used a handkerchief from her bag to dry her eyes.

"I'd just gotten my sister back when she was taken away. Papa needed me, and all of a sudden so did you."

She looked up at me with her mascara streaked down her cheeks.

"And now, the both of you seem bent on leaving me with no one."

She put her head against my chest, and I petted her hair. I felt her choking back tears. I rubbed her back and her hand fell into my lap and again I felt the sensation of arousal. This was Liana's sister for Christ's sake. The woman I'd been told was nothing but trouble since I'd met her.

I cleared my throat. "I saw your boss the other night."

"Who? Ludo?"

"At a cabaret."

She shrugged nonplussed. "He has business all over town."

"Do you know what he did during the war?" I asked.

The door opened again, and Zelie came in. Alix pulled herself together and sat up.

"I'm sorry. I didn't mean to interrupt," Zelie said, standing in the middle of the room.

Alix started to say something, but caught herself. I should have introduced Zelie as my newly adopted niece and explained how she was tied to Liana, but I just asked how her night was instead.

Zelie didn't answer, she looked at Alix and then walked down the hall to her room. Alix got up and ran her hands down her skirt.

"I should go."

"It's fine, you can stay."

"It's late."

She started to the door. I pushed myself off the couch and followed.

She gave me a look. "I'll ring next time."

"No need, really."

She looked down the hallway. "Un peu jeune, n'est-ce pas?"

And then she was gone. I listened to her heels clicking down the stairs. I thought Zelie might come back out, but she didn't.

In the morning I braced myself for the Embassy with a double espresso.

Sylvia, the first secretary's receptionist, informed me the boss wasn't in. She glanced over to the red cushioned chairs.

"Can you ring me in my office?" I asked with a toothy smile.

"Of course," she answered. "Anything for Gregory Peck."

I laughed. Maybe it was true I looked like the actor when we had first met. But not anymore.

I made my way down the back stairs to the basement and almost as far back into the bowels of the Embassy as one could go. I unlocked my door and flipped the lights. It smelled of vacancy and paper. Lots of paper. It seemed like an eternity had passed.

I sat behind the desk and recalled my old life. What would be for dinner? Would we go out? Take a walk? But that was when this office was organized, brighter somehow.

Now it looked like how I felt these last two years. A little prison cell.

While Liana was being murdered, I sat here, pushing papers, making calls. It had been the ambassador himself who'd knocked lightly on the door, his face saying everything. "There's been a tragedy," my tragedy.

The phone jingled and I answered it.

"The first secretary will see you now."

"Thanks, Sylvia."

Upstairs I was ushered into Robert Carlson's plush office. He shook my hand and patted me on the back.

"Good of you to stop in, Eli. You're looking great."

"Thank you, sir."

"Have a seat. Can I get you a whiskey?"

"No, thank you."

Carlson looked a little uncertain, diverted from the bar to behind his desk. He took his pipe from the desktop and spent some time getting it started.

"We weren't expecting you back. But I'm glad to see you looking well."

There was something in his tone. There was news, and he hadn't planned on letting me in on it yet.

"Well, I'm doing much better and was hoping to get back to my duties, sir."

There was that uncertainty again in his gaze.

"Glad to hear you're on the mend. We always appreciated your good work for the Embassy."

I felt a lump in my throat.

"You remember Bill Colman?" he went on. "Friend of yours from the Third, I believe."

"Before that even. Ol' Bill," I said, knowing what was coming.

"Well, he'll be here in only a few days' time. Going to help out with visa applications, as well as keeping an ear to the pavement. Keep tabs on all the Soviets making hay here in Paris."

My job in other words, I almost said. "Bill's a good man. But I expected to return to my duties as soon as things..." I didn't even know how to finish. When I was done having a nervous breakdown?

"Perhaps there was a misunderstanding. I thought it was understood you'd be heading back stateside soon. Won't it be nice to be closer to your family? A safe government job back home?"

I hadn't thought through the realities of returning. Had Ambassador Dillon secured some administrative job for me at the post office or Department of Labor?

"Well, I'd certainly understand if that's how it's to be, sir. But I'd really prefer taking up my duties again here."

Carlson's face was full of sympathy and maybe some of it was sincere. He gave me an appraising look.

"Afraid the wheels are in motion, Eli. Your reassignment's already in the pipeline. But tell you what, why not spend a little time with Bill? Catch him up on his duties here. It'll give you a little time to get used the idea of heading home."

He tapped out his pipe.

"Thank you, sir. Happy to show Bill the ropes."

"Great. You're a team player. Take another couple days. Bill's reporting next week."

Carlson stood, held his pipe in his left hand and shook

mine with his right. He seemed to be in deep thought and didn't let go of my hand for a couple beats.

"Actually, maybe you could help us out with something that's come up. You're the only one who's dealt with something like this before."

"I'd be glad to help," I said, knowing any assignment might keep me in Paris longer.

"A Russian wants a quick exit to the States. A liaison officer with the French Communist Party. They usually only get a one-year placement you know. This one isn't keen on going back behind the Iron Curtain. Entrusted his life with Tommy down in filing. Must have noticed him coming out of the Embassy and then either by chance or plan met him in the bathroom of a bar, La République Populaire. We had his photo in the Russian binder, but no name. The note he handed our man only had a drawing of a bear. He said he would return the same time on Saturday."

"That's just a couple days away."

"I know. I was going to send Carl, but he has no experience with this kind of thing. And he doesn't have your knack for intuiting a man's true loyalties."

I considered the irony of what the First Secretary had just said. "Thank you, sir. I'll meet him and let you know if it feels legit. Then I'll set up another meet to test him on what he might have to offer us. Carl can handle whisking him off to the airport."

"Good, good. Glad you can do this stint for us."

"I appreciate it, sir." I turned to leave. "Oh," I said reversing course. "One last thing, First Secretary. The Gestapo files left in Paris after liberation. Do the French have them?"

He smiled and returned to his desk. "Rumor is they're

piled up in the Hotel de Soubise. But if you ask the French they'll deny it. I have no doubt someday, 30 years from now, they'll suddenly turn up for everyone to look at. But until then, they don't officially exist."

"What I figured, sir. Thanks."

On the way out, Sylvia gave me a conspiratorial wink. I had just bought myself some time.

Chapter Four

JP DIDN'T WAKE ME UP. The smell of coffee did. My head hurt. I lifted it off my arm and sat up on the couch. Liana's papers were scattered across the floor like a bomb had gone off. JP came out of the kitchen and leaned in the doorway. He looked agitated. As if his daughter's ashes were carelessly spread around the room.

I grabbed a handful of papers and brought over a box to put them in.

"Don't bother with that now," he said, turning back into the kitchen.

I got up, grabbed the whiskey bottle and made my way through the papers to the kitchen. My head was pounding. JP was looking out the window and I took the opportunity to pour what was left in the bottle into the mug of coffee he had poured for me.

I took a drink and looked around the kitchen for a pack of cigarettes. Nothing. Only an ashtray with stubbed out butts on the table. Had Zelie been up already?

"Wait here a second, I want to show you a photograph Liana was keeping at her office."

I went to my room, slid the photo out from my jacket pocket and grabbed a pack of smokes off the bureau.

While JP looked at the picture I lit up. I was starting to feel human again.

"It was under a false bottom in her desk drawer," I said. "He was a professor at the Sorbonne, taken away by the Gestapo and never seen again. On the back is the date and address of where it was taken. October 3, '42. Not in Liana's hand."

"So maybe she never knew about it, maybe it belonged to whoever had the office before her."

"That would have been him," I said, tapping the photo.

"Did you check out this address?"

"Not yet."

"Might tell you why it was taken in the first place." JP handed the photo back to me and opened the terrace door. "What's it mean? Does it tie in?"

"I don't know," I admitted.

JP snorted and walked out. I took my coffee and followed him onto the balcony. As I closed the door Zelie came into the kitchen. Maybe if she saw I had company she'd have enough sense to go back to her room.

JP looked out over the balustrade letting his cigarette burn between his fingers. We weren't making much progress and he knew it. There was a short rap on the glass and then Zelie came out with a coffee mug. At least she was fully dressed. I made the introductions.

"Alix mentioned you had a teenager living here," JP said with a sardonic look.

"This is Osval's stepdaughter," I said. "She's helping with our investigation."

"Is she now," JP said, turning to face her. "And what have you found out, little lady?"

"That Osval was having an affair," she replied, unfazed by JP's sarcasm. "With a man."

JP pulled a face. "Not just in America anymore."

"It's something," I said.

"Is it? You think someone killed Osval for being a pervert?"

"I don't know. Could have been another lover. Could have been someone from work."

"Wasn't he a machinist?"

"Also a PNU party member," I said.

JP was offended. "I'm a PNU party member!"

"I know you are. And look how you reacted to Osval's private life."

"That's how any Christian would react."

"But what if we've been looking in the wrong place? If the communists *weren't* responsible. His own organization was. Someone disgusted by who he was."

JP took another drink and thought on it.

"There's a rumor," he started and then hesitated, taking a drag on his cigarette instead.

"Rumor of what?"

He looked at me hard and then pursed his lips.

"Come on!" I barked.

"That there's a splinter group in the party. Diehards. The ones that do any dirty work that needs doing."

"People that might kill to keep its membership pure of 'perverts'?"

JP's brows lifted. "I have no idea. Seems like a long shot."

"It's a lead even if it's a slim one. Zelie and I talked to the man Osval was having relations with, but he didn't tell us anything useful, other than maybe someone Osval knew saw them together and it spooked him."

"Maybe I could poke around," JP said. "Someone might know something about this secret group."

"Be careful. Everyone knows you, knows what happened to your daughter."

"And that I hate the communists for it. That's why I joined the party in the first place. The only reason."

"There's something else. Also, maybe nothing," I cautioned. "But when I went to Zelie's work, her so-called uncle was outside. Anyway, I think it was him. He'd followed me or followed her. I don't know."

JP soaked this in. "You should be careful."

"So, we'll both be careful."

JP smiled. "Yes. I still say it was that bastard Siméon Lamar. He didn't pull the trigger, but he ordered it. That's good enough for me."

Siméon Lamar, the Paris head of the Communist Party, had been JP's suspect number one since the start. But neither us nor the police could find any connection between him and Osval's murder.

"We went over and over that route two years ago," I said.

"I know, but he's a clever bastard," JP groused. "Keeping that lot of rabble together. He had something to do with it, I know he did."

While I drank my coffee, something occurred to me. "I think we might have a way of finding out," I said. "But you can't say a word to anyone. It's life or death."

"Tell me."

I looked over at Zelie.

"Who am I going to tell?" she cried.

I shook my head. "Official government business."

"Fine," she said, glaring. "It's not like I'm any help."

She pushed open the door and slammed it behind her. Luckily the glass didn't come crashing out.

JP shook his head and laughed. "She's got your number." He lit another cigarette. "Now what's your big idea?"

"We have a defector," I said, leaning in. "A Russian wants to come over. He works with Siméon as a go between with the Kremlin. We can use him."

JP hit the railing with his fist and gave me a sly look. "Have the Russian defector congratulate Siméon for having Osval killed, one less dirty PNU henchman in the world. Then see how he reacts."

"Maybe two years ago," I dismissed. "But this Russian wasn't even stationed in Paris then."

"Okay, so something else happens," JP persisted. "Something this defector could blame on the PNU and suggest that they were finally getting even for Siméon killing Osval."

"Like what?" I asked.

"I don't know," JP said, throwing up his hands. "Something."

We both contemplated while finishing our cigarettes.

"How about some more of that coffee," JP said. I took his cup inside and poured in the rest of the coffee. I wasn't sure I liked where this new line of thought was heading.

"Look," JP said, when I handed him the cup. "It sounds crazy but hear me out. We kidnap someone important in the French Communist Party. We hide them away a few days, and then you have the Russian defector do his bit." JP paused to drink his coffee. "He could even produce a note from the kidnappers, something that says straight out – 'We've killed *so and so* in retribution for Osval's death.' Simple."

I couldn't help but laugh.

"It's not as crazy as you think," JP said.

"It is, actually," I replied. "And I'll only agree to it if the communist we kidnap is that asshole Philippe."

JP smirked. "He'd recognize our voices. Anyways, I already have someone better. *His* girlfriend. She's also in the Party, heads their committee on women's rights."

"Known to Siméon?" I asked.

"She's more important than Philippe," he said.

"Except," I said, less certain of my own mind. "She doesn't deserve it."

"No," he replied. "But sometimes you pay for the sins of others."

This plan was sounding worse by the minute.

"Look," I said, trying to figure another way. "Maybe the defector knows if the Russians or the Paris Communists killed Osval and Liana. He might. If not, then we can revisit this harebrained scheme."

"Okay, okay," JP conceded. "If you think you can trust what he says. But, if not, I have access to chloroform. After some unpleasantness we can take her to my nephew's farm in the country."

"Henri and Cosette's?"

"If she raises hell, nobody will hear her in Burgundy."

"What will *they* say?" I asked.

"That I've gone stark raving mad, but Henri will do it."

"Nuts," I said.

JP moved in front of the glass door. "It will only be a few days, right? I'll stay with her. After you and the Russian defector meet with Siméon, I'll pack her into the van and drop her somewhere on the riverfront. She'll be no worse for wear."

I shook my head. "Let's wait and see what the Russian can tell us."

"Ok, but think about it, this should be done." He stabbed out his cigarette.

I followed him back through the kitchen. He gave the living room another sweeping look.

"I'll have all this put back," I said.

JP just took a deep breath and let himself out.

I spent the next half hour putting papers and books and notebooks back into boxes. There was nothing. Nothing to suggest Liana was a communist, or trying to track someone down, or having an affair.

Only that she had beautiful handwriting, wrote biting comments about art critics, male ones for the most part, and was brilliant. I didn't have to read every essay to know her mind contemplated art in a way I barely grasped. What I couldn't understand, I felt. The creative process, the meaning of it, was air to her. The purpose of understanding ourselves through our creations or what we hoped to create.

I didn't know if it was important to her or not that I finally understood this about her. She never came home and talked to me about what she was writing. She showed me her artwork when I came to shows, let me get from it what I could without comment. And I was always proud of her no matter how bizarre I thought something looked or made me feel. Either she thought I was too dumb to understand, or she didn't need me for that. She didn't need my encourage-ment or protection there.

Chapter Five

THAT AFTERNOON I REPORTED TO THE EMBASSY. There was nothing to do but I wanted to be seen sober, and back on the job. On Saturday I hung around the apartment, sitting on the porch drinking coffee and trying not to think about Liana. I'd spent two years thinking about my dead wife. Now I had the added weight of thinking of her with him, what they did with each other while I lived in blissful ignorance.

When the sun sank below the building across the street, I knew it was time to go meet the Russian. The bar wasn't far, a twenty-minute walk. I didn't know if I should feel nervous or not. These defections sometimes went wrong. But people left Russia all the time, it just depended on if the KGB cared and if we wanted him or not. A liaison officer might cause some alarm if he didn't report in.

Helping him didn't feel like a priority given everything else, but he might be useful in getting a confession out of Siméon. JP's kidnapping idea was insane but could work. It depended on how motivated our Russian defector was. Hell, this whole defection could be some Kremlin ruse to see how we handled it. A test for when the Soviets really slammed the door. Everyone knew it was coming. Two years ago, restrictions were put in place to keep all the young and educated from abandoning the commie ship.

The cool evening air kept me in the right frame of mind. There was no sense getting worked up. I'd just have to listen to what my gut told me. I'd dressed as if I were going to play cards with my father-in-law's friends and hadn't shaved. It felt good to walk through the Tuileries wearing thick-soled boots, the sound and feel of them against the cobbles was satisfying. I noticed again all the young people about. Spring was the season French women loved the most, when they cast off the pale of winter and wore dresses that drove men crazy with desire. I caught myself looking at a pair of long legs walking past. How had I managed not to notice these last two years? Did I feel less connected to Liana now because of her affair? I didn't think so. If anything, I was bound to her more than ever. She was everything I'd done wrong, every mistake that drove her away, the reason I was on this hunt.

I was fifteen minutes early. I stood outside and smoked a cigarette. It was naive of me to think I'd just know, that my intuition would tell me if this Russian was sincere about defecting. But I'd give him a test. The answer I'd been looking for might be what got him on a plane to the U.S.A.

I stubbed out the Gauloises and pushed open the door. It was smoky inside. A Charles Trenet song was playing. It was mostly men but a few women too. There was nothing special about this bar. The crowd was "end of workday," a potent mix of tobacco, grease, oil and sweat. I ordered a Pernod at the bar. There was no one that fit the description of the Russian. And nobody that looked like his minder. While I waited, I skimmed the daily *Le Monde* someone had left on the bar. The Radical Party's leader Pierre Mendes France was favored to be the next Prime Minister. The country was sick of fighting in Indochina and he had promised to get them out. I couldn't blame them. Almost a hundred thousand Frenchmen had been killed over there.

I'd just finished my second Pernod when a well-coifed man came in. He sat at the bar and ordered Smirnoff. His accent did not surprise the bartender. No doubt other Russians came into this proletarian bar now and again. He looked over at me and then looked back over the bar. He drank his vodka in the usual way, one gulp, and then made his way to the restroom. I folded the paper and started to the front door. On the way I pretended to have a sudden urge to urinate before I left and turned back.

The Russian was looking into the cloudy mirror while he washed his hands. I pulled his note from my back pocket and put his bear drawing on the sink. He picked it up, tore it into little pieces and washed them down the drain.

"We will need you to do something for us."

He nodded once.

"Siméon Lamar?"

Again, a nod.

"Are you being watched?"

"I don't think so," he frowned. None of them ever really knew.

"Can we meet somewhere else?"

"The Great Sphinx at the Louvre. Wednesday at 4:00."

I looked him over and then pushed open the door. Something told me he was legit. His nerves were for what he was about to do with his life, not what he was doing for the state. Of course, I could be wrong. Maybe they'd sweat that out of him later.

I put a call to JP's Union and left a message that we

should talk more on Tuesday about bringing Belle to the country ball. That was three days away.

On Monday morning I went to my office and found Bill Colman sitting in the chair in the corner. At least he wasn't behind my desk. He bounded up and shook my hand while slapping my other shoulder.

"Christ it's been a long time," he said showing a healthy smile.

"Great to see you, Bill," I said sincerely even though he was here for my job. "How are things stateside?"

"All hands on deck, every penny spent countering the Reds," he replied with just a hint of sarcasm.

"It's the same here," I said, giving him another pat on the back. "Staying fit?"

"No," he laughed. "But I've started racquetball. Don't suppose they have it in Paree?"

"You might find some indoor soccer," I said, wondering what the hell racquetball was.

"Sorry again about Liana," he said.

"I appreciated your letter."

"I don't know how you got through. It would just put me over."

"It may have," I said. "Did you bring your family?"

"They're coming. In a few weeks from now, when the kids are out of school for summer."

"Good thinking."

"You'll like Katherine, she's a sweetheart. We would have all been great friends, I'm sure."

I nodded with the tightlipped smile I'd become used to giving when I heard condolences.

"I suppose you know why you're here?"

"I didn't when I got the offer. Believe me, if I'd known I'd've turned them down."

"It's alright. I didn't give them much of a choice."

"Will you go back to the States?" he asked.

"It's hard to imagine being back home. I haven't seen my family since they came over on the Queen E four years ago."

"I'm sure they'd love to have you."

"Yeah," I said. But I wasn't so sure. No doubt everyone would expect me to find another wife and have kids before I got any older.

"Hell, I'm not even supposed to report in until Thursday," Bill said with renewed cheer. "Why don't we get a drink and catch up. Can you get out?"

"Showing you the ropes is my only assignment. So let's get you familiar with the local bars."

Bill laughed heartily and shook me by the shoulders. "Damn, it's good to see you, Eli."

"I'm glad you're here," I said, feeling suddenly emotional. I sucked it in with a deep breath. I had no defenses anymore — Liana had knocked them out of me.

Outside the Embassy it was just getting sunny. It was too early for the usual places. I hailed a cab and had him bring us to Harry's on rue Daunou.

"An American bar?" Bill asked with a laugh.

"We need to ease you into French life," I replied. "This is every American's first stop in Paris. Who knows, maybe a sentimental Hemingway will stop in."

For the first two highballs Bill filled me in on his demobbing, his job for the CIA and Allen Dulles. Then a move to the State Department.

"I didn't care for the life of a spy, especially one that just sat at a desk," he said. Then he caught me up with his wife and kids. "They met Truman you know." He looked embarrassed for bragging.

"What was the old man like?"

"You wouldn't have believed he dropped the bombs. It was just a quick photo op. I told him it was an honor to meet him. He said the honor was his."

"Well, I'm sure he was briefed on your having single-handedly liberated Paris."

"I had a friend," he said, finishing his drink and ordering two more.

Drinks three and four brought us to my life in Paris. I told him about Liana's death and how I pretty much became useless at work. I had completely fallen apart.

Bill ordered two more.

"Before we get too skunked here," I said, feeling pretty unsteady, "I can bring us to the Select, Le Dôme, le Ritz bar..."

"I never leave a good bar unless I'm being kicked out," he replied. He got off his stool. "Need a piss."

I nodded and toyed with my coaster. It had a sketch of a fly sitting on a cube of sugar. I shredded it while wondering if I should tell Bill about what JP and I were up too. But knowing what we were planning might be a liability for him down the road.

The drinks arrived when Bill came back and we progressed.

"And what about since? Are you dating? How are you keeping sane?"

"She can't be replaced, so what would be the point?"

"Just to keep on living. She'd have wanted that, wouldn't she?"

"I don't know," I said. "I really don't."

Bill put an arm around my shoulders. "Well, I do," he said without elaborating.

Telling Bill the news about Liana and Philippe would have put a curve in the conversation. It would probably be good to talk to Bill about it. Get a man's perspective. But I kept it in. I knew once I started, there'd be no stopping. I pushed it all down, deep into my gut. Was it shame? I wondered as I lit a cigarette. Did I not want him to know I'd been fooled so badly? That some part of my marriage was a sham, even though I couldn't quite say what part that was. Did I really need other people to think I'd had it great with Liana? That she had been the faultless wife I'd always made her out to be? Would people stop pitying me for her death if they knew what she'd done?

Somewhere along the way, my ability for serious conversation was lost and our evening turned into a laughing, red-faced, back-slapping recount of old times. High school crushes, pranks, stories I hadn't heard or told in too long.

In the morning Zelie was in my bed. I lifted my head and looked down. I was still dressed, minus tie and shoes. I slipped my legs over the side of the bed and tried to sit up. A chainsaw was buzzing through my skull. Zelie slipped over and sat beside me.

"You were crying," she said, her hand on mine. "Not normal crying. You couldn't stop, you couldn't breathe. I was scared for you."

I didn't remember, but Bill had removed every roadblock. I wasn't surprised.

"Was Bill here?"

"No, you came home alone. I held you, but I don't think you knew I was here."

"I'm sorry," I said, holding my head.

"I'm just glad you're okay." She stood. "I'll go get you some water."

"Thanks," I managed and lay down.

Zelie picked up my legs and pushed them back onto the bed. Poor girl. Probably scared the piss out of her.

I spent the day in bed. Zelie sat with me and brought up the paper and made tea. I knew I was supposed to meet JP to talk over our kidnapping scheme but couldn't get myself moving. We'd have to put that whole thing off a day if we actually went through with it.

Zelie played gin with me until work. She picked up the game fast and beat me more times than not. She came into my room in her work outfit before she left and gave me a sultry look. What was a girl as caring and thoughtful as Zelie doing at a place like Le Coq?

I managed to make my way to the kitchen and ate a chunk of cheese and piece of bread. Out on the porch I could see young revelers heading out to more lively parts of town. I wasn't sure I missed all that or not. Going out with Liana was not the same as going out with GIs on leave. Those nights were hectic and goal driven. To get a girl to have a drink with you and maybe a kiss in the dark afterward. More if you were lucky.

Being with Liana was serenity. My beautiful French girl on my arm. I was to be envied, or I imagined I was. To sit across from her at dinner was to have no worries. Everything was ahead. Everything was the golden tint of her hair.

Had she stolen that from me with her affair? Affairs? Were there others who didn't need envy me? Others who laughed at me behind my back? How could she have done that? Made me a fool.

I smoked a cigarette and looked up at the sky. She'd left me the stars at least. Or were they spoiled too? Was my life ruined now that I knew? I felt somehow that I could save it all. There was some way I could turn a switch in my head and everything would be precious again. Everything still beautiful about our lives together. But I had no idea how. And being conscious that I had no idea sat heavily on my heart.

Tomorrow I would meet the Russian defector and future American, and also maybe kidnap Philippe's girlfriend. A busy day. I smiled at the absurdity.

I'm a fucking idiot, I thought. But the path led this way. I had to follow. What did I hope to find in the end? Would vengeance grant me absolution? Would I have Liana's forgiveness for being the kind of man who couldn't keep her safe? Would I find peace when her killer was dead? I wanted a drink but smoked another cigarette instead.

My thoughts drifted to the four months Liana and I spent apart after the war, when the army sent me back to the States. I was so full of anxiety that I'd never get back to Paris I could hardly sleep at night. I was sure I'd be stationed in Timbuktu. The only comfort I had was Liana's letters. Her devotion gave me hope.

When my former Intelligence CO pulled some strings to get me the Embassy posting I was ecstatic. There were just a couple of "conditions." The first was I had to agree to be part of "Eisenhower's Army," the secret plan to have

Americans in France for the purpose of countering a Russian invasion. Since that seemed unlikely, the risk was low. The second was filing intelligence reports. The idea of relaying what I might overhear at parties or information coming directly from traitors and informants gave me a bad taste. But at the time, I didn't care if my job was emptying the trash. I just wanted to get back to Liana.

Chapter Six

WHEN I GOT TO THE LOUVRE, the Russian wasn't at the Sphinx, so I wandered into a gallery of French paintings. I recognized Francois Desportes. Who wouldn't want a room-sized painting of hunting dogs tearing apart a stag on their wall? Further on was a gallery of Jackson Pollock. Liana had been advocating for an exhibit of his work for years.

Would her glass tree look out of place here? I didn't think so. She was an incredible artist even if she had turned out to be a shit wife. And really, she'd been a good wife. I didn't know how to square it anymore.

It was ten-after. I got back to the Sphinx and found the Russian looking intently at some ancient gold coins. He looked over at me.

"We have train cars of such coins. Not Egyptian, but treasures of other countries we've made our own."

"Too bad you don't have any," I said.

"Yes, too bad. I would have to share them with my fellow workers, of course," he chuckled.

I smiled, indulging his Soviet humor. He looked around. There was no one. I had checked the other rooms to make sure we were alone.

"Tell me what it is you need."

"There was a right-wing agitator killed here two years

ago. Osval Delage. We think your people ordered it or Siméon Lamar did."

He looked at me with something like disbelief. Or maybe it was relief. "This is it?"

"We need the truth. We have a good idea, so answer with great care."

He shrugged. "I sense that you don't, but I will still tell you the truth. My predecessor told me a war was raging between the political parties of France and that our job was to fan the flames. He told me there was an incident, a PNU provocateur and a bystander had been killed in the street, and that we were under suspicion by the French government. I usually wouldn't have asked such a delicate question from a Soviet official, but he was someone I had known for years. His answer was: We didn't do it. And that I should be careful."

I was looking into his eyes. He laughed. "You want some proof? I can't get any. But I can tell you that this man, Osval, was part of a splinter group in the PNU party. A gang of nationalist thugs terrorizing France's various other liberal parties. We had a file on it."

"Can I see it?"

"If I go back to Russia, maybe I could take a look before I get put on a train to Siberia. But maybe not."

Typical Russian.

"My people want you to do something for Uncle Sam before he opens his arms to you in welcome. We need something to corroborate this. What's your name?"

"I am Sergei. And there's nothing I can do. If I ask the wrong person, I'll be arrested before you can get me on a plane."

I took Sergei's arm and walked him into the next room. I didn't know what to think except I believed him. Fuck. Believing him wasn't good enough. Then I had a thought that beat the whole kidnapping thing.

"I'll settle for you introducing me to Siméon. Then you ask him a couple of questions about Osval's death."

"Your people suspect Siméon?"

I nodded.

"It would be a very bold move on his part, especially without sanction from the Kremlin."

"Will you do it?" I asked.

He put his fingers to his chin looking dubious but made a begrudging sideways nod.

"If you say nothing, which would not be uncommon for a Russian attaché brought for reasons of intimidation."

"Then you probe him while I listen. I think that will be proof enough for my government."

Sergei shrugged. "Fine. But I will need to be out of the country before Siméon thinks to ask someone who you are."

"I will arrange it. When can we meet him?"

"On Monday."

"Fine. Oh, and Sergei, if anything sounds cooked up, I'll know."

"I doubt that," he scoffed. "Le Cheval Rouge is around the corner from Siméon's office at 44 rue Le Peletier. Meet me there at 3:00, and wear a trench coat, leather if you have one."

I nodded. "On Tuesday you will meet another contact. The password will be 'Fool's Luck.' He will meet you right here at 5:00. And bring your toothbrush, you won't be going back to your room."

"I will. Thank you." He shook my hand harder than anyone else I remember. "Thank you, thank you, thank you."

"See you Monday," I said, pulling my arm back from his.

I left him, going deeper into the Egyptian rooms. By the time I circled back Sergei was gone.

I waited outside JP's Union a half hour before I saw him park his van across the street. He got out quickly and tilted his head at me to follow. I caught up with him outside his bar, Le Chien Paresseux. He pulled me inside by the elbow.

We took a table and I could tell JP was excited about something.

"What gives?" I asked.

"First, tell me if the Russian admitted to anything."

"He said the Kremlin had nothing to do with it."

JP snorted. "Horseshit."

"Maybe. But I have a plan to find out, and the best part is…" I lowered my voice, "we don't need to kidnap anyone. He's going to introduce me to Siméon as an attaché, and then question him about Osval's murder. Simple, right?"

JP looked like I'd just sucker punched him.

"Merde," he croaked.

"What's wrong?" I asked. "This saves us a lot of trouble."

JP still looked like he'd run over my cat.

"It's done, it's already done," he said, dropping his head into his hands.

"What is?"

"The girl. She's already at my nephew's!"

"Jesus Christ, Jean-Paul, we were supposed to talk about this!"

"I know, but I had the opportunity and it's not what

you think. I didn't have to lay a finger on her. But I told her about you and what happened. You will need to speak to her. It was her only condition for going along."

"What the fuck are you talking about?"

"I'd been following her for days," JP said. "To get ideas about where best to grab her. This afternoon, it was beautiful, was it not? She went to the Jardin du Luxembourg, sat down and took out a book. That's when I thought of it. She might go away willingly if she knew what a prick Philippe had been. I sat down next to her, introduced myself."

JP stopped, leaned back and looked at me sheepishly.

"And what?"

"And I told her the truth," he spat. "About Liana's affair with her boyfriend and how you want to break Philippe's legs."

I shook my head. "Christ almighty. I'll have the flicks at my door."

"It's not like that. I also told her how Philippe kept key evidence about my murdered daughter from the Sûreté. I said all you wanted was him to feel some of the pain you did. If she'd go away a few days, you wouldn't hurt him."

"And she agreed to this?"

"She was pissed. They've been together four years and she moved in a year ago. The affair does not surprise her, but she was still pissed. She said she'd do it if you would come get her when the time was up. She wants to talk to you."

"I bet she does. You know you might have screwed everything up."

"Yes, but I didn't. And now she's at Henri's safe and sound. I brought her there, just now."

I leaned back and took out my cigarettes. JP took out his lighter and we both lit up.

How could we use this? Should I tell Sergei to mention the disappearance to Siméon? It seemed pointless. One more cog that might cause confusion or get someone hurt.

I exhaled tobacco smoke and noted an unusual satisfaction in doing so.

I looked across at JP who was looking down at the table, the cigarette ash crawling quickly to his lips.

"And you don't think she'll call Philippe and let him in on the game?"

JP met my eyes and smiled.

"My nephew said he would hide the phone. And Mia, that's the girl's name, promised not to, as long as *you* met her. She's willing to let Philippe blow in the wind for three days."

I smiled at JP despite myself. At least the asshole would feel some pain. That was something.

"What's next?" I asked.

JP shrugged. "I keep telling people I'm out for commie blood. Maybe a door will open to this goon squad."

"Or you'll end up arrested."

He started tapping his pack of Gauloises against his palm.

"I haven't been to Henri and Cosette's in years," I said. "Liana loved it there."

"I know she did," he said. "They'll be expecting you Saturday. Don't forget."

I patted my breast pocket for scrap paper and found the photo I'd been carrying around. This would be a good time to check out the address on the back.

JP chuckled to himself.

"What?"

"Nothing," he coughed. "Good luck with the girl."

"Thanks," I said, leaving out "Wise-ass."

On the sidewalk I took another look at the man in the photo. I guessed he was in his late 20s. Good looking, his whole life ahead of him.

A life with Liana?

What had he been to her? Just a mentor? Or was there more to it? Had she hoped they would be together when she graduated?

I didn't know and probably never would. Unless he was still alive somehow. Could he have been the informant? Had the Gestapo taken him away publicly to erase suspicion of him? Alois said he was never seen again. Not even as a corpse?

At the Jardins du Palais Royal I took a right on Richelieu. I found rue St. Augustin and walked west two blocks before coming to 36. It was definitely the place. The white door in the picture was black now, but the brickwork on either side was the same. I crossed the street to get the perspective of the photographer. There was a narrow alley between two buildings. There was a gate, but there may not have been in '42. I looked back at the doorway. The photo was taken from here, and by someone who did not want to be seen.

I crossed back over and knocked on the door. After a minute a young woman came out. But she was not answering, just on her way somewhere.

I asked if the landlady was in.

She opened the door wider and pointed to the door on the first floor. "Madame Brodeur."

My interview with *la patronne* lasted about two minutes.

She claimed work never ceased for her, but my guess was she had no interest in reminiscing about the war. She told me the basement had been used by the Resistance as a meeting place and that her mother had been severally beaten and imprisoned for it by the Gestapo. I thanked her and got back outside.

It was a sunny spring day and as I got closer to the Louvre the sidewalks became clogged with tourists. American GIs, now with young families, took in the sights and lied to the wife about what they had done in Paris during the war.

Something about the sun on my face or maybe the fresh air reminded me of the trip Liana and I had taken to Graubunden and St. Moritz. It was our last summer together. I had never seen anything so beautiful.

We had spent a few nights camping at the base of Piz Nair. It was our first time in a tent together. Our lives had become so enmeshed in Paris we had forgotten the world outside it.

Something ignited between us that week among the heather and flocks of sheep grazing on the alpine clover. I realized on that trip that I would never grow tired of Liana. Our lifetimes wouldn't be enough for all the new experiences ahead. What did it mean that this monumental trip had been but a short break in her affair with Philippe? How could it be that she had returned to him after sharing that place with me? Maybe it was time to admit that I was always going to lose her; I was never going to be enough.

But what *might have been* was meaningless. What *did* happen required justice. And even if Alix was right, that Liana would've wanted mercy for her killers — that was too fucking bad.

Chapter Seven

THE COUNTRYSIDE AROUND SENS WAS MOSTLY FARMS and rolling hills. A region known for expensive wines and my favorite French meal, beef bourguignon. JP's van wasn't exactly a "deuce and a half" but it reminded me of hauling supplies to the line before I moved to intelligence. The brass was desperate for interpreters. I spoke German, something I'd kept from the draft board, but when I intervened in a shouting match between prisoners I went from truck driver to interrogator, and then to forward reconnaissance when they also discovered I spoke French.

I guess everything worked out the way it had to. I wouldn't have met Liana otherwise. And even now I knew I could never regret that.

The road curved along a hillside pasture and on the other side I could see Henri and Cosette's brick farmhouse, a place of unspoiled memories. I stopped the van before the driveway to take a few deep breaths. The last time I'd visited was to spread Liana's ashes.

I parked beside the barn and met Henri coming out from the house. We hugged and laughed like long-lost brothers. Cosette kissed both my cheeks and pulled me into a tight embrace.

"It's great to see you," she said, choking up.

I managed to keep it together, mostly, and we spent five minutes catching up on the past two years.

"Ready to meet your prisoner?" Henri asked at the sound of the screen door.

When the woman, Mia, reached us she gave both Henri and Cosette hugs and warm goodbyes. I guessed that drinking wine and playing Napoleon for a few days hadn't been all bad. I didn't know how to greet her.

"Will you walk with me?" she asked.

"Yes, of course," I said.

Henri smirked and followed Cosette to the house.

We started down the drive.

"I owe you an apology," I started.

"For putting a hole in my perfectly indifferent life?" she asked in good English.

"Yes. Among other things."

"Would I have preferred ignorance? I would have. Maybe you would have too." She gave me a wistful look.

I noticed the fullness of her, the ruddy complexion and long, dusty hair. She was not the thin, delicate Parisian type. Her ancestors had been of heartier stock, the freckled peasantry of France's countryside. I had a vague thought of her dancing on Bastille Day.

"Your father told me you had plans to break Philippe's legs. Is that true?"

"My *father-in-law*. Yes, the thought has occurred to me."

"The deal was if I did this, you wouldn't do that."

I nodded. She started down the cart path between fields.

"What should I say when I get back?"

"That you were kidnapped," I told her. I didn't want Philippe blaming her for willingly going along with our crazy plan. "You were kept in a room in the countryside and don't know why."

"Okay," she said. "Will this help you?"

I didn't want her thinking she sacrificed for nothing. "Yes," I said. "I think so."

"He will hurt, you know. Some anyways. He'll worry. And it will pain him to think I've left him."

"Will you?" I asked. "Leave him?"

"No," she said without thinking. "Would you have?"

"I don't know."

"You haven't forgiven her?"

"No," I answered. "But you will?"

"Yes, I'll have to. He is good for me."

I thought maybe she could do better but didn't say it. She looked down at the dirt path.

"Do you want to sleep with me?" she asked. "Will that help you forgive?"

"I won't forgive him. But I won't hurt him now. You don't have to worry," I said.

"It will not give you pleasure, being with me?"

I had no doubt it would give me pleasure.

"It would have hurt Liana, I think. I would have liked that. But I can't hurt her now. Only the other way around."

"I understand. But I will still do it if you want." She smiled at me and added, "You're handsome in your own broken-down way. And he was not faithful. Why should I be?"

I looked over at her. She was giving me an opportunity for tangible vengeance. But she wouldn't tell Philippe. I knew that much about her. And neither would I. So the vengeance would just be in my head. And as cute and pleasant as she seemed to be, I felt no affection for her, it would be just an act. It would not be the emotional bond Liana must have made with Philippe. It would not be love. That was the part that hurt the most. The thought she had made room for someone else in her heart. Sleeping with Mia would change nothing.

"If it will help you," I said, stumbling.

She shook her head. "I only offer for you. I don't want you to hurt him. I want you to keep your word. I will let you fuck me if that will help you."

It was a strange conversation. One only a French person could have. I thanked her for her thoughtfulness. She stopped and took a few steps to climb up onto the stonewall. She looked over the pasture.

"I need to come out to the countryside more often," she said. "Paris is beautiful. But I forget this."

She held a hand out to me. I thought about how some GI had probably clambered over this wall, hoping he wouldn't get shot on the other side.

I took her hand and stepped up onto the wall.

"You were in the war?" she asked. "You saw men die?"

I managed to nod.

"Then you know life is short. It is cliché to say, even in France. But it's true. You should forgive her. She did what she did. The reasons are too many and too few to understand. Don't try. You loved her?"

She looked at me. I nodded again.

"Could you have been wrong? Could love have been wrong? It couldn't be."

She held my hand and we both looked back toward the

farmhouse. A dog barked. The road home was just a few feet away. She squeezed my hand.

"I don't know you," she went on. "You and your *father-in-law* took something away from me. Not just three days, but the something you lost after you found out. A naive belief in love, its honesty. I never really believed in it. But sometimes I pretended too. Now I can't. I know you did not mean to hurt me. I did nothing to you. But now that you have, I want you to let this go. Philippe wronged you. He deserves what you have given him. He deserves to find out I've been unfaithful. Maybe someday I will give him that pain too. But now, I'm begging you to leave it."

She squeezed my hand tighter and I saw the pained look on her face.

What would I have done to protect Liana from being hurt? Anything. I would have died to save her. But I could do nothing now. Nothing to prove my devotion to her like Mia was doing for Philippe.

"For you. I promise."

She wrapped her arms around me. The rocks shifted, but we kept our balance. I felt the penetrating warmth of her. Philippe was lucky. He was a fool and so was Liana. It was a carousel that never stopped going around. There was never a reason. We would never understand it. And it would keep coming around. It would keep asking the same question. I would keep trying to answer it, for the rest of my life.

She rubbed her eyes with her hand and stepped down from the wall. I followed and we walked back up the dirt path.

"We're never going to see each other again," she said.

"Is there anything about what happened you want to tell someone?"

She was giving me an opportunity. I thought about my night out with Bill, how I'd kept it all in. I could tell Mia how hurt I felt, how betrayed, how much I resented Liana for humiliating me. But it had lately boiled down to something else.

"I didn't think anyone could understand the love we had," I somehow managed to say out loud. "Not our parents, our friends, no one. Turns out it wasn't so special after all."

She took my hand. We started walking again.

"You're wrong. It's the reason you hurt like this, and I don't."

After letting Mia off near the Jardin I drove the van over to JP's and climbed the stairs to the third floor. I hadn't been there in years. It's where Liana lived when we met.

"How did it go?" he asked, closing the door behind me.

"Fine. Your nephew says he 'forgives you.' The truth is I think they liked having her as a houseguest. She's a special kind of woman."

"I thought so too. She reminded me of Myriam before the war, tough and beautiful."

His ex-wife was still those things.

"I meant to tell you," I said. "I went to the address on the back of the photograph. The landlady confirmed that the Resistance met there during the war."

"So, somebody follows this young professor, snaps a photo and rats him out."

"Looks like it," I said.

JP smacked his fist. "Then why did Liana have the damn thing?"

"I've no idea."

The apartment looked just as I remembered it. The walls, the carpet, the table, the giant radio, everything as it had been in happier times.

JP went to his bedroom for cigarettes, and I visited Liana's old room. We hadn't spent much time here. When we courted and things had heated up, she had come to my billet. But we sat here, on her bed, and talked about what was to come. My departure for America, my promise to return. JP hadn't moved much around. Emilienne probably stayed here when she visited. It looked lived in. I noticed the same yellow comforter on the bed. Somehow it still cast a warm color over the whole room. I wanted to smile and cry at the same time. I knew I'd need to get out of here. Too many memories were collapsing on my head.

JP's door clicked and I took a last look around and followed him down the hall to the kitchen. He went to the icebox and took out a glass bottle of seltzer. Then poured two whiskeys.

"To our Liana," he said.

I tapped his glass with mine. "To Liana."

Chapter Eight

ON MONDAY MORNING I MET SERGEI at the café but was already having misgivings. I didn't have a trench coat. The best I could do was a black leather jacket that I'd had in the closet from who knows when.

The six-story building that housed the headquarters of the Comité Central du Parti Communiste Français looked octagonal from the front and was covered in tan tiles. There was a huge banner hung from the top floor that read: "*Yes to a Sovereign Constituent Assembly.*" I knew that the communists felt underrepresented in the French legislature. The place was being patrolled by tough-looking youths who looked at me with open hostility.

"Ignore them," Sergei said as he led me inside. "Their job is to intimidate protestors."

The man at the security desk just nodded at Sergei and we took the stairs to the third floor. Siméon's secretary sent us in to his office, which was large and spartan. When Siméon came in he shook Sergei's hand jovially while he kissed his cheeks. When he shook my hand, I detected a slight hesitation. He moved behind his desk and Sergei introduced me as a visiting attaché to the Soviet Embassy in Paris.

Siméon looked at me but did not reply. He folded his

hands on his desk, making a peak with his two pointer fingers, and turned to Sergei.

"Moscow is using American intelligence agents as attachés? How strange."

Sergei laughed. "Of course not, comrade."

Siméon made a downward motion with his hands. "It's okay, my friend. Whatever you're up to, it's your own head. I'm not the Kremlin."

Sergei looked like he might fall over. He managed to slump into one of the red chairs.

Siméon stood up and came around to lean on the front of his desk. "And you, Mr. Cole. I think I know what brings you here. Frankly, I expected you a long time ago. I heard plenty about you hounding my men. Even spreading rumors that *I* had something to do with your wife's death."

At that he came within a foot of me and looked me in the eyes. "The truth is, I probably did have some part in it." He turned and went back behind his desk. "But... not in the way you're thinking."

Sergei stood up now and said that perhaps it was best if he left us alone. He gave me a slight nod, a question without words, and I gave him a nod back. He turned to Siméon but only managed to say "Poka." Siméon gave him a genuine smile and replied, "Udachi."

Sergei managed a tightlipped smile and left the room.

"I won't ask," Siméon said, shaking his head.

"Better that way," I answered. "But Sergei was just being sympathetic."

"I'm sure," Siméon dismissed. "If you had come to me right away, I would have told you everything I knew about Liana's death. But instead, my men were rounded up by the police for interrogation, others beaten by PNU thugs using Osval's death as an excuse. These things happened because you were shaking the tree to see who fell out."

"You had the most to gain by his death," I replied.

"And yet, it wasn't us." He sat back down and indicated the chair to my right. "Did you know your wife was doing some party work?"

I nodded.

"Don't worry, she was not spying on you. She made that very clear. Of course, we hoped maybe someday that might change," he admitted. "No, she wanted to start an arts collective, promote artists and writers of our particular political bent. That was her main goal, but in the meantime, I gave her small jobs to do. One of them was to go to opposition rallies."

I remembered the orange flier for the PNU rally among her papers.

"I'm listening."

"At one of these rallies she told me she recognized someone from the occupation. Someone she thought might have betrayed a professor of hers, who was killed by the Gestapo. She wanted to find out. She needed help proving her suspicion."

"She asked you?"

"Despite what you might think of me and the party, I was in the Resistance. And not just at the end when it was convenient to do so. The communists paid the biggest price in France for fighting the Nazis. Ironically, the majority of the activities preceding the American landing on D-Day were perpetrated by the communists you now all loathe so much."

I didn't want Siméon to get sidetracked. "The Resistance is held in high regard by my country, I assure you."

He gave me a cynical look. "I did some digging. I found a Gestapo agent who'd been stationed in Paris at that time who wasn't dead or hiding in South America. He had been arrested, not for the crimes he committed during the war, but for a subsequent murder in Germany. And I found a member of the same resistance group her professor was part of. I gave her both their names. I don't know what, if anything, she did with the information. But I've always felt somehow it ended up getting her killed."

I felt suddenly sure that he was right.

"Did she say who it was, the man she saw at the rally?"

"She didn't give a name. She wanted to be certain first. Only I gathered it was someone from the Sorbonne. A professor perhaps."

"You'll write down those names?"

Siméon nodded and took a folder from his desk drawer. He copied out some information.

I stood when he came around the desk to hand it to me.

"I am sorry," he said. "She was well liked here."

He put out his hand and I took it. "Thank you."

"Just be careful," he said, giving me a sympathetic look.

"What about Sergei?" I said. "Can you give him a day?"

"I don't even recall him coming in."

I didn't have much choice other than to believe him.

Outside his office I looked at the paper he'd handed me. Remy Meyette and Ernst Werner, along with last known addresses. A million thoughts were fighting for my attention as I turned toward the stairs. But for now, finding these men had to be my first concern.

*

When I got back home, I found Zelie sitting in the kitchen smoking. Without her makeup she looked like the young woman she was. My lovely, neglected niece.

"Have you found your man?" she asked coyly.

"Not even close," I said, opening the patio door.

She followed me out and leaned against the balustrade. She was wearing one of my undershirts.

"Yannick was at the club again. He watched me from the bar. I almost told Pierre to bounce him, but didn't."

"Best not to antagonize him."

"He's letting me know I haven't gotten away, not really."

"Has he followed you here?"

"I don't think so, but he'll figure it out." She stubbed out her cigarette using her bare foot. "And I'm bored. You're never here, my friends think I'm whoring..."

"What?"

"Well, someone probably saw me going to work. I guess it's true. That's what you think, isn't it?"

"No, it's not!" I said. "You've got goals and you're making your own way to realizing them. What's wrong with that? Besides, no niece of mine would do such a thing."

She burst out laughing. After drying her tears, she gave me a hug and didn't immediately let go. She had unexpected strength. I pried her off and went back into the kitchen and pulled a bottle of Pierre out of the fridge.

Zelie sat back down at the table and pulled another cigarette from the Lucky box.

"Hey," I said. "Take it easy on those. You'll be a raspy old woman."

She cut her eyes at me.

I took a swig and looked at Zelie. The girl could get into trouble. It would be better for everyone if she was occupied with something. Anything to keep her busy.

"Do you want to help?" I asked, knowing I'd probably regret it later.

She looked up like I'd just handed her a puppy.

"I'm looking for someone. I need to ask him some questions."

She stood up and put the cigarette back in the box.

"Who is he?" she asked. "Wait!" She ran out and came back with a small diary and pen.

I gave her Remy's name and last known address.

"The woman who lives there now hasn't a clue. I stopped on the way home. She said her friend Gina lived there before her and before that Gina's aunt. Now dead. But maybe I had the wrong apartment."

She scribbled everything down.

"Did you ask anyone else living in the building about him?"

"Nobody was in."

"And why do you want him? What questions?"

"I just need you to find him, Zelie. I'll ask him the questions."

"Fine, but just so I know."

"You don't need to know."

She looked at me with fury in her eyes and slammed the notebook on the table.

"I need to know what NOT to say to people! Someone's going to want to know why I'm looking for him."

"Fine, it's about someone he may have known during the war. A traitor. Or maybe not a traitor. I don't know. But I think he can help me find out who killed my wife. Tell people he's your long-lost uncle or something."

"Another uncle?" she smiled. "I have too many already."

She folded up the notebook and went off to her room. I took the cigarette back out from the box and lit it. I knew my next move was to get to Germany and question this Gestapo thug, Ernst Warner. Maybe he knew the collaborator who betrayed Liana's professor. I'd need Bill to cover for me a couple days.

In five minutes, Zelie was back in the kitchen, dressed in a schoolgirl uniform.

"I'll talk to you in the morning," she said.

"Your disguise is convincing, but don't you have work tonight?"

"This *is* for work," she said.

Jesus.

Chapter Nine

TEN PACKS OF LUCKY STRIKES was the price set by prisoner Werner, lieutenant of the Paris Gestapo, for agreeing to meet me. It would be a small fortune. My request to visit with the prisoner had taken almost a week to be cleared, then the demand for cigarettes came a day before I left by train for Berlin. I'd debriefed JP on the meeting with Siméon. He didn't like the part where Siméon claimed not to know who killed Liana and Osval. He was still suspicious of him even though it turned out he'd helped her with information.

"Maybe helping himself a little more," he'd said.

Bill didn't ask too many questions before agreeing to cover for my absence. Now that Sergei was on his way to America, my situation at the Embassy depended on Bill vouching for my usefulness. He also let me buy a wad of dollars off him in exchange for francs.

"Occupied Germany?" he asked.

I just smiled and waved the bills at him.

Berlin was not how I remembered it. There were people going out, new buildings, big block-shaped apartment complexes, kids playing in the street.

Nightlife, which had been famously libertarian during Weimar, was drifting back in that direction. The night I arrived I walked into the Charlottenburg section on Paulsborner Strasse and headed toward Tiergarten Park. Loud jazz emanated from basement clubs, young people stood outside the entrances smoking cigarettes and trying to look cool. I had a Heineken at a bar with an English band.

If there was an after party following some stuffy Embassy to-do, the record on the player was usually Duke Ellington, Benny Goodman or Glenn Miller. These kids probably never heard of them. I felt out of place, an invader. At least there were some American soldiers cavorting about. Germany was still occupied after all. But there were rumors that would be changing soon. Another year? Two?

I almost headed back to my room but decided to have a drink at the Zoo Hotel. It was maybe a little too ritzy, but I'd had a glass of champagne there in '45, so felt nostalgic.

There was something about being away, especially alone, that made me want to visit the center of sin. I could wander Place Pigalle in Paris of course. The young people and clubs were in full swing in my own adopted city. But for some reason I never did. I had gone to London on my own for a couple nights while Liana stayed home. I did the same thing. Walked around Soho, ignored the come-ons from prostitutes, had a beer in a bar that was too loud to think and then drifted back to my room.

There was a difference this time. But the end would be the same, wouldn't it? These kids had each other and if they were feeling adventurous there were plenty of GIs to seduce. They didn't look twice at a 40-year-old American out of uniform.

The walk to the Zoo Hotel was pleasant. It was a cool evening and the stretch across the British Sector intermixed between quiet, dark streets to wide avenues and finally the famous Kurfurstendamm. The wide boulevard was Berlin's answer to the Champs-Elysees, with shops, restaurants and cafés, once the haunts of celebrated writers. What would the Germans do when it was all back in their own hands? I hoped they wouldn't turn the clock back. This was Germany's future. This generation. Mine was fading away, becoming irrelevant, even as we held all the strings. Liana knew that. She knew our music, art and social norms were stifling the younger generation. There would be a revolution, eventually.

The bar was busy and even in my blue blazer I felt underdressed. I found a stool at the bar and regretted coming in. I should have just taken a look inside for old time's sake, remembered that drink at the start of the occupation, and then walked back.

I ordered an old fashioned. How appropriate.

The crowd here was the old guard. My people. I would have preferred mixing with the kids at the jazz bars. But we all belonged to our own generation I supposed. What could be done about it? I'd have to stick it out the best I could.

A rather elegant woman stood beside me and ordered a martini. She was the epitome of German womanhood. A frank looking face, with shoulder-length blond hair. Her emerald green eyes assessed me while she waited. She was wearing a silky black dress that dipped low at her neck and hinted at curves and soft skin beneath.

In my current place in life she was way out of my league. When the bartender returned with her martini, he gave me a look. It said *Watch Out*. Was she a professional? I decided to find out. When she pulled a cigarette from a pack in her purse I took out my Zippo.

She offered the tip of her cigarette to me, bringing her face ever so close to mine. She inhaled deeply and let smoke drift from the side of her mouth as she lifted her head.

"Danke," she said.

"Willkommen."

She took a drink and turned back to me.

"American?"

I nodded.

"Let me guess. Here on business."

"Afraid so."

"Where would Germany be without all her new friends?" She smiled to let me know an answer was not expected. "And your family, you brought them along?"

"Divorced," I said.

"Nothing is easy, is it?"

I shook my head and took a long drink.

She looked around the room to give me a moment to appreciate her shoulders, the diamond earrings, the expertly applied black eyeliner and dark lipstick and the small beauty mark on her cheek.

When she brought her eyes back to me she seemed to be asking if I'd seen enough.

"Do you stay at the Zoo?"

For a quick second I considered getting a room. Then registered the absurdity of that and said, "No."

"But close by?" she prompted, finishing her drink and leaving the glass on the bar. She licked her lips and then headed toward the door.

I lost an ice-cube down my shirt. Then, not knowing

exactly what I was doing, put five dollars on the bar and slid off the stool.

She was talking to a cabby through the passenger side window. Was that to give me a minute to make up my mind?

I opened the back door and she got inside. But not all the way. When I sat down, she leaned against me, putting her head on my shoulder. The cab pulled out from the curb. I gave him the name of my hotel.

Her hand slid onto my lap and her face turned upward, offering her lush lips, which sparkled with the lights of Berlin.

I got to Plotzensee Prison early. Instead of waiting a half hour inside I had the cabby take me to the closest café. It was a residential neighborhood, so we had to go about five blocks.

I sipped an Americano and noticed for the tenth time that morning a soreness in my neck and lower back. Who knew a couple of years of celibacy would make me feel like I'd just run a marathon. Martina's tall and youthful body was everything the dress had advertised. She had been intent but not in a hurry. Afterwards she smoked a cigarette by the window and gave me, as perhaps a bonus, the pleasure of seeing her awash in the whitish glow of the streetlamp. I had not been surprised when she bent toward me sitting on the bed and whispered, "100 Marks." About twenty-five dollars. I took out three tens from my wallet and left them on the nightstand. She smiled at me, kissed my cheek and went out the door.

Our hour together had cost as much as the hotel and ticket to Berlin. But it wasn't just the unexpected aches I was feeling this morning. I felt like I used to when fall weather arrived and school was about to start. The way I felt on VE Day when I understood I wasn't going to die in this god-forsaken war. What the feeling meant exactly I wasn't sure. What had changed other than the end of a two-year vigil?

I'd had opportunities before now. A year ago, I'd concluded sleeping with another woman would not be a betrayal of Liana. It had been something else. My desire was extinguished. And now? Was some flame being rekindled?

I knew I wouldn't get another cab, so I finished my Americano and jelly blintz and started walking back to the prison.

The interview room was eggshell blue and clean, not the dingy cell I'd expected. No doubt American dollars had been spent updating this place. Two guards brought Ernst Werner in leg shackles and sat him down across from me at the metal table.

"You brought the cigarettes?" he said in German.

I pulled five packs from each jacket pocket and pushed them across to him in a stack. I regretted giving the bastard the pleasure of American tobacco but kept any resentment from my face. I wanted him to think I didn't care one way or the other about him or the information I needed. Just another cog doing his job for the U.S. Government.

He pulled a pack open hungrily and put a cigarette to his mouth, looking at me for a light.

I tossed a book of matches over to him and he lit up, inhaling deeply and with great pleasure. He probably had just such a look when pulling people's fingernails out. It was hideous.

Then the glint that had shown in his eyes with the first inhale became dull again.

He must've hated being the one in irons now. The Nazi fuck.

"I need to ask you a few questions," I told him in German. "The longer we talk, the longer you can smoke in peace and not worry about someone stealing from you."

He smirked. "There is order here."

Even in shackles he espoused the superiority of German discipline.

I shrugged. "You were stationed in Paris in the fall of 1942, at 11 rue de Saussaies?"

"You know I was."

I took the picture of Gael Favret from my breast pocket and watched him carefully as I slid it across the table. He didn't look at it.

"What is in it for me?"

I looked at the stack of Lucky Strikes.

"More," he said.

"If you help."

He looked at me hard and then relaxed a bit. He picked up the picture. The cold stare did not hide recognition.

"Do you know him?"

"What if I do? I'm not copping to anything."

"But he was a prisoner? Someone you... saw?"

"I didn't say that."

"Is he alive?"

He said nothing. The cigarette was almost all ash. He let it burn right to his fingers.

"You can buy cigarettes here?"

He nodded.

"Ten U.S. dollars. Three questions."

"Depends." He dropped the cigarette on the table and pulled another one from the pack.

"Was he a Gestapo informant? Is he dead?"

"What's the third?" he asked.

"On a different subject."

He opened the book of matches and did not look up. He took his time sliding the match over the flint.

"I won't tell you how I knew him. Only that I've seen him before. I will answer your questions."

He lifted an eyebrow and I reached for my wallet and put the ten-dollar bill in the middle of the table.

"He was not one of us," he said, pocketing the cash.

He lit his cigarette before the match burnt his fingers and considered how to best answer the second question.

"I happen to know from sources I will not divulge that this man died at the end of 1942."

"I have a date," I bluffed. "Confirm it."

He tried not to show the workings of reconstructing the event. "I don't know the exact date, it was early November."

That was when Alois said Gael had been taken away.

"And the last question?"

"You had an informant at the Sorbonne," I started. "Keeping tabs on fellow academics."

"What of it," he shrugged.

"I need a name."

His eyes went to the ceiling. "Not my department. I only knew someone was well placed."

"You never met? Never saw his file?"

He returned his gaze to me and shook his head.

I didn't want to look at the scumbag for another second.

I stood up and went to the door and knocked. The guard outside peered in and opened the door.

I heard Werner laugh as I turned down the corridor. He laughed and laughed until I was through the next set of doors and then the sound of the only power left to him was cut short.

On the train back to Paris I felt more at ease than when I was going the other direction. Werner had confirmed that Gael was not an informant. He also corroborated what Siméon had said about Liana suspecting someone as a collaborator at the Sorbonne. If Gael was with the Resistance then the photo that Liana had must have come from another informant or a Gestapo agent. If that were true how the hell did Liana end up with it? And was that answer what started her looking into his murder? Did someone give it to her after the war? Who?

How else might she have come across the photo? I needed to know who her friends were while she was at school, or if she worked for anyone. The only person I could think to ask was Alix. How frustrating. This could very well be an impossible problem. Add that to the impossibility of accepting Liana's death, the impossibility of accepting her infidelity, and now finding the professor's killer, finding Liana's killer, and knowing what to do if I ever did.

I opened the bottle of schnapps I had bought at the Berlin Friedrichstrasse station and took a swig. I had nothing to celebrate, but it was close to the tenth anniversary of D-Day and getting shit-faced on a train had its advantages. There was very little trouble to get into and it killed the time.

I rolled my coat under my head and looked out the window. It would be too dark to see anything but my reflection soon. We followed a road, but there were very few cars. Telephone poles became a rhythm and I closed my eyes. I hadn't gone back to the Zoo Hotel bar for Martina last night. Why? Wouldn't she have been expecting me? Where had the doubt come from?

I imagined seeing her in the company of another man. His arm around her, Martina smiling at just the right moment. Better not to see that. She was a professional after all. She had no feelings for me one way or the other. The fact that I had a warm and grateful feeling toward her was a testament to how lonely I was.

The doubt won out in the end. I had a very good wienerschnitzel and beer at a biergarten close to the hotel and watched the nightlife parade by. The women in Berlin did not disappoint. But even as I thought it, I knew it was the same everywhere. Paris, London, even small college towns in New England. Beautiful women walking by and all of them dreaming of a man who wasn't me. Except maybe, I thought whimsically, some Berlin escort wondered a brief moment why the American had not come back for a second night. I smiled to myself. Even that was pretty unlikely.

The dining car served dinner two hours before we were due in Paris. I had a hamburger and fries, which was not something I got much in the city. I had a Budweiser and considered my watch. Would it be too unexpected to show up at Alix's apartment at ten? She might be entertaining after all.

There was a line for cabs outside Gare de L'Est so I started down Magenta Boulevard toward Place de la République. The air was cool but refreshing and it was nice to use my legs again. By the time I got to the statue of Marianne I was wide awake. I buzzed Alix's apartment and heard the window on the fourth floor open. She stuck her head out and gave me a quizzical look.

"Can I come up?" I asked.

"Bien sur," she replied.

The door buzzed and I pushed it open.

"Were you sleeping?" I asked when she opened her door in a glossy robe.

"It's been known to happen from time to time."

I put my bag down. "Sorry. I just got back from Berlin."

"I thought maybe you were moving in."

The apartment was warm. Alix closed the door and went to the bar.

"Whiskey?"

"Do you have soda water?"

"Yes, I'll get you some."

Alix brought over the whiskey sodas and set them on the glass table.

She sat down next to me. Her left leg was exposed up to her inner thigh and I did my best not to notice.

I was suddenly unsure of what I was doing. If I got right to business Alix might be offended. I asked her how things were going.

"Is that why you came over? I was worried you were going to try and seduce me."

I took a drink and smiled at her.

She smiled back in a way that told me nothing.

"I need to know who Liana's friends were at school. She got this picture somehow."

I showed Alix the photograph of Gael. "And I need to know from who."

"Liana had very few friends and kept them to herself.

Everyone was too busy surviving for friends. And, God forbid, they might want something from you."

Alix to a tee. I didn't think Liana would have felt the same way.

"What about work? Did she have a job?"

"If Liana was working it must have been for a pittance. She wasn't buying extra food or new shoes."

I put the picture back in my pocket.

"I've never heard you talk about the occupation," I baited.

"That's because everything my sister told you was true. I did *consort* with the enemy." She took a drink. I said nothing, hoping she would go on.

"It seemed so terribly unfair that I'd have to walk around looking like a boiled ham when the day before I'd been head girl at Le Bon Marche's cosmetic counter. I was scared," she said, glancing over at me. "I didn't think I'd be able to live like everyone else. I needed more. It didn't take long for me to get noticed. And I didn't fight it. I wanted champagne and clubs. I would have died huddled around the coal furnace at home."

"Like Liana?"

"Like everyone. Papa broke his back slaving for the Boch. I wanted *him* to get something out of it. One daughter taken care of by those pigs he served. I knew my sister seethed. But I helped her too. When I got chocolate, Liana got chocolate. When I got nylons, she got them."

She had become flustered and now breathed evenly. "I thought she would forgive me for all of it when I found you. The day they shaved my head and covered me in shit, I begged you to save my sister. Not me, my sister. The only evidence they had of her *collaboration* was what I had given her. But she never forgave me, for any of it, until she lowered herself to my level. In her eyes I was always just a cheat."

Alix pushed herself up and went to the bar. She poured a large glass and drank standing with her hand on the countertop.

"But we'd see you at family dinners. You always seemed okay together," I said, trying to soothe her.

"It was always there," she replied. "After the war she didn't approve of my friends. I was keeping the books for a black marketer. Another way I fed the family during shortages."

"An accountant?" I said, surprised.

"The government tried shutting us down while at the same time making us necessary. Anyone living on just rations wasn't going to live long."

"Is that how you met Ludo?"

"Yes, but he didn't ask me to work for him until a couple years ago. The job seemed a lot more exciting than numbers."

"But just a little dangerous," I nettled.

"I run a discreet establishment for his friends. There's little risk there."

"There's always risk when you associate yourself with people like Ludo. Didn't you just spend some time *away* because of him?"

She tightened the sash on her robe and a chill entered her voice.

"Don't think you know me, Eli, just because my perfect, wait, *not so perfect* sister told you tales. I do what I have to."

"I could have helped, you know," I said. "If you'd asked."

Alix snorted. "And listen to Liana lecture me on never doing anything for myself? Not a chance."

"She loved you," I said. "She told me many times even if she never showed it."

Alix poured a smaller glass and came back to the couch. "I loved her too. When we were kids we kept each other's secrets and defended each other at school. Somehow we needed each other back then."

"She still needs you."

"By helping you and Papa on your crusade? I told you she wouldn't want it."

I decided not to push. She leaned her head back on the cushion and closed her eyes in frustration. I couldn't help but take the opportunity to look her over. The silky robe was doing very little to hide the soft, inviting beauty underneath. I'd wondered before if Alix's good looks had caused tension. What if your sister always got the boy, always got everyone's attention? But what did that have to do with anything now? Alix was just being herself.

"There's something different about you," she said. She put her glass down on the table and moved closer to me.

I gave a nervous shrug.

Her hand went to my neck and brushed my ear. "We're not the same woman you know."

She was very close now, her breath was sweet with whiskey. I felt the tension in her fingertips as they gently pulled me to her lips. Her mouth opened to mine and I was immediately lost in the lush intensity of our kiss.

There were many reasons I didn't want this to happen but they got no traction. In a moment her robe fell from her shoulders and my hands found her full breasts. She unbuttoned me and we fell together to the floor. I was engulfed in the heat of her body. When we finished, the warm crest of pleasure quickly melted to regret and shame.

Maybe Alix noticed the change. She pulled the robe around her as she stood and went to the bathroom. I pulled up my shorts and slacks and fixed myself. When she came back out she had a drink from her whiskey and sat down in the chair. I sipped the whiskey and said nothing.

After a minute she leaned to me and kissed my cheek. Then she moved down the hall.

I sat another minute on the couch feeling like an idiot. Then gulped my drink and went out the front door.

Dim light glowed from JP's apartment window as I walked by. I decided to push the buzzer.

Upstairs he poured us drinks. Not that I needed one.

"All the Gestapo thug told me was that Gael was dead and hadn't been working for them. Claimed they had an informant at the Sorbonne but didn't know his name."

"Great," JP replied sourly.

"But knowing it was probably someone at the university Liana had recognized at the rally is helpful. I'll ask the old professor if he knows anything tomorrow."

"And the other guy, the Resistance fighter?" JP asked.

"Still looking," I answered.

JP lit a Gauloises and pushed the pack over to me.

"Any luck with the PNU goon squad?" I asked through the smoke.

"I've been grumbling at meetings that we never do anything about the commie menace. That they killed my daughter and got away with it. I think maybe somebody's finally noticed."

"Why?"

"Because I'm being kicked around like a football," JP said with a laugh. "*You want to get back at the commies? Talk to this guy.* Then he'll tell me to see someone else. They're waiting for something. The right time to use me or a time to get rid of me, one or the other."

"Or maybe both," I said.

JP chuckled again. "Could be. This last guy I talked to, old army type. I get the feeling he's the one we're looking for."

"Who is he?"

"Pascal Venier. Not an officer in the party, but somehow you just know he's pulling the strings."

"Have you asked him about Osval?"

"Not yet, but he wants me to meet some big wig political donor who shares my distaste for communists. Has some huge estate out in Arques-la-Bataille."

JP finished the little glass of Suze he'd been nursing and got up. "You should take Alix out sometime. I think she's been lonely."

I nearly choked on my drink.

He patted my shoulder. "I'll stop by in a couple days."

Chapter Ten

IN THE MORNING I TAPPED LIGHTLY on Zelie's door but she didn't answer. Usually, I'd hear her come home in the wee hours, but I must have been sound asleep.

I walked out into the morning sun and climbed the hill to the Sorbonne. Courtemanche's class schedule was conveniently tacked on the wall beside his office door. He was teaching now in a classroom a floor below and wasn't scheduled to be out for another hour. I took the stairs down a floor and peered through the foggy windowpane of Classroom 120. He was there, in front of a small group of students, maybe a dozen, lecturing from a fat textbook. He didn't look up.

I patted my coat pocket for my lock pick and then headed to the building with the faculty gallery. No one was around, so I slipped inside without a hitch. I flipped on the lights and looked in wonder at the imposing glass tree. How was it that Liana had made this and never told me? Had she intended for me to listen to it someday?

I pulled out the drawer and rewound the tape to the beginning. I pressed play and sat down on the floor.

"Love, time, the distance, sun, father, like fallen, coat, me, beauty, under…"

After two minutes I clicked it off. I rewound it again

and pushed the drawer in. The humming sound of the tree somehow seemed to make more sense. This was how it was intended to be heard, like keys being played on an ancient instrument. I sat back down and closed my eyes. If it were an instrument, then the words had meaning. Just like music-al notes did.

After ten minutes I pulled the drawer out again and rewound it.

"Time, ours, home, lives, forest, run, Paris..." Why was it all so familiar? Like something I'd read before, words I'd seen or heard Liana say. "Apart, ocean..."

The cadence, the way she was reading, it was like...

When it hit me, a sudden heat swelled inside my chest and spread to the rest of my body. Liana's letters. I'd heard this voice in my head as I read them all those years ago.

I stopped the tape. A flood of emotion enveloped me like an embrace. I bowed my head and cried.

By the time I got back to Alois's office my head was swimming. What I'd just listened to was Liana's love letters transformed into a new language. The sounds of that love *must* have been a message she hoped I'd someday hear.

I knocked on the professor's door and tried to collect myself.

"Come in," he answered.

When I sat down, I could tell something was off. Alois gave me a stern look and offered no welcome.

"I have a couple of questions," I said, feeling like a policeman.

"And I for you," he said hotly. "Liana told me you were

'most likely a spy,' but that doesn't give you the right to kidnap my friend and colleague."

I was speechless. I felt like I'd just been plunked down in the principal's office.

"Did you know Mia was faculty here?"

"That whole thing was a mistake," I explained.

"I doubt it," he said. "Philippe was quite unnerved when he told me. You have him scared to death."

"Well..." I started.

"I know about Liana's affair, that's still no excuse."

I felt flush.

Alois looked down and took a couple of calming breaths.

"Everyone knew, didn't they?" I asked.

"Not everyone. When I picked up on it, I told her it was not good for the department."

"When was this?" I asked.

Alois shook his head. "Shortly before she died."

I took out my cigarettes. Alois got out of his chair and opened the window. He used a handkerchief to blow his nose.

"Schnapps?"

"No, thank you," I said.

"I'm sorry, Eli. I know this has been hard on you."

"Look," I said, not wanting to give away the game, "the kidnapping was meant to shake up Philippe. Mia was always perfectly safe."

Alois nodded. "That's reassuring. But still..."

He poured himself a drink and left the rest unsaid. He looked very old.

"Have you considered that you know the answers?" he

asked. "All the questions you have about her affair. The clues to these things are always there if you look."

I met his eyes a moment. "I've been trying not to."

He nodded and didn't speak again until his teacup was empty. "What was it you wanted to ask?"

I tossed my butt out the window. "I found out from a German prisoner that the Gestapo had an informant at the Sorbonne. I thought maybe you knew who it was."

He shook his head. "I mean, I'm not surprised. But whoever it was, it's not common knowledge."

"What about anyone who flew the coop after liberation?"

Alois rubbed his forehead in thought. "I remember there was an administrator in the art department, we all wondered if something had happened to him. The day the Germans marched out, he was never seen again."

"Remember his name?"

"Gustave," he said. "Gustave Dubroc. Quiet fellow."

"Would Liana have known him?"

"Possibly. There were clerical jobs students took upstairs. The pay was nothing, but the little extra line on a transcript might be helpful later on."

"Liana had a job like that?"

"I've no idea," he confessed.

The clock behind his desk chimed and Alois put his bottle away. "I have to go," he said.

"Remember what he looked like?" I asked, standing.

"Vaguely," Alois replied. "Average height, fair haired, late 30s I'd guess."

He led me out to the busy hallway and locked his door. "Don't fight the tide," he smiled.

At the stairwell he waved over his shoulder, and I poured out the front door with the student horde. I wondered if any of these kids knew what awaited them in a few years' time. When their friends all went off in different directions, and they found themselves walking down this sidewalk alone.

At a payphone I dialed the number for the Embassy. The operator connected me to Donovan in records. I asked him for anything we had on a Gustave Dubroc. If he was still alive, maybe he had a perfectly legitimate reason for disappearing from the Sorbonne after liberation.

"Where are you?" Donovan asked. "I'll call you back in an hour."

I gave him the number for Le Carré Rouge, where I sat at my usual table. Ames, the waiter outside, brought me a water and I ordered an Ouzo.

I thought about what the professor had said. Could I retrace my steps and find where things started to go wrong? I tried placing everything back the way it was during that last year. I was 37. Alix was living at home along with her mother and sister. Liana was at the height of her career. She had gallery shows and an agent who occasionally sold her work overseas. I remember it being a fat time for both of us. We were making decent money, and there was no end to the cocktail parties. Liana's were usually bohemian affairs, and mine more formal. Our schedules were full, we saw each other in the evenings, most evenings anyways. A chat about our day over dinner, some wine during the radio show, and then a pleasant fuck if we weren't too tired.

My Ouzo arrived and I lit a cigarette. For some reason my mind slid back to the rush of students at the Sorbonne. A brief moment of belonging and purpose. What was it like for Liana to be part of such an ocean of youth and all their causes? Anti-war activism, labor strikes, civil rights, feminism. No wonder creativity filled her up, she was surrounded by the fuel of inspiration.

I looked down at my cigarette and then the pack on the table. Gauloises. I must have swapped packs with JP somehow. The thought of JP smoking Lucky Strikes and noting the superiority of American tobacco made me smirk. I knew the realization would irritate him.

I wasn't sure I could replay a year of our lives together. Even if I did would anything stand out? She was obviously very good at keeping things from me. Did I ever notice if she came home agitated? Was she ever so distracted by something that I took note? It was possible. I would need to really submerge myself to remember the details of all those nights. There had to be a better way to get through those memories than a bottle of whiskey. But what would Liana have wanted me to see that I'd missed?

Ames brought a phone out to the table.

"Eli," I heard Donovan say when I picked up the receiver.

"Go ahead."

"Nothing doing. Your Gustave Dubroc is a ghost."

"Okay, thanks."

I walked home in the shade of early evening and brought some bread and cheese out to the porch. I had hoped to catch Zelie but she must have already left for work.

It wasn't that I wanted to forget the last year of my marriage. I knew all my memories of Liana were precious. I could picture her at one of those artist parties, leaning against the wall, a bottle of Pelforth in her hand, and a smile to reassure me that she was mine. I even remembered talking to Philippe at one of them. He seemed like a decent guy, the asshole.

How many times did I think that she was too good for me? Too smart, too beautiful, too youthful.

I remember admitting once to her that I didn't know why she loved me. But she replied that her love only grew the longer we were together. And I believed her. And I still did, somehow.

The tears that came were not in a rush. They just blurred my eyes until I wiped them away. I went back inside and didn't bother with a glass. I just took the Threlfall's to the couch and lit a cigarette and let myself get lost.

"Should I go down and hail a cab?"

Liana came out of the bedroom holding shoes in her hand. "I thought we'd walk. I'm wearing flats."

"They're in the cinquième? Your friends?"

She nodded and went into the kitchen. I followed her and watched as she fastened the straps sitting at the table. When she finished she bounded up and into my arms, giving me a tight hug and kiss on the lips.

"I think you're going to like Raul and Esmee. *She's* ten years older than him. They're madly in love and both of them are wonderful painters."

"And he's from Mexico?"

"Cuba, darling. Cuba."

"Right. Let's meet these lovebirds."

She kissed my cheek, leaving her lips there, standing on her tip toes until I smiled and kissed her back.

We held hands as we walked. We always held hands. On the occasions I walked with her to school we always clung to each other like we'd just met. And if I held her around the waist or around her shoulders we walked in rhythm. I knew it meant something that we were so attuned with each other.

It was satisfying not to have to let her go today. We passed La Petite Chaise and I wondered why I kept forgetting to make reservations.

Liana's friends lived in a first-floor apartment that had a trellis over the back door. Their kitchen was full of sun and they poured sangria and showed us a dummy copy of the book they were working on together.

"We are making only ten copies," Raul said in Latin-accented French.

"It is diary entries and serigraphs. We are doing all the pressing at the studio."

It was a colorful, folio-sized book on thick handmade paper. I had a feeling Liana wanted a copy but I had no desire to ask what the price might be. Or even if one would be for sale.

Esmee took Liana's arm and led her and us out under the trellis to their tiny yard. Raul took off his wire glasses and put them in the V of his shirt. He had thick black wavy hair that I was sure he never combed, the kind of mess that only looked good on the young. I guessed he was twenty. She had short, bleached hair and was wearing suede slacks and a men's t-shirt. Only her eyes hinted at her age. They were a beautiful couple.

I wondered if anyone saw Liana and I the same way. As we stood in the evening sun I admired Liana's youthful face and body. The ten years I had on her was no doubt easily read in the lines on my face and the widening of my mid-section. I thought of us as a handsome couple, but what did her friends think? I had never cared until this moment. Did Liana want to be as lovely together as they were?

Later, Esmee made us *ropa vieja* served in red and yellow ceramic bowls. I sat on the bench at the table and watched as Raul cut oranges into a pitcher of red sangria. The three artists leaning against the kitchen counters as they ate and talked and laughed. Their excitement for one another was electric. I could see it in Liana's glowing face.

I could have joined them for cigarettes outside in the gathering dusk, but I stood in the doorway and listened to the fragments of their *joie de vivre*.

By the time we left my confidence had ebbed low.

We walked home despite the light chill of evening.

"We're lucky," I said hopefully, squeezing her waist. "To be so in love."

"The luckiest," Liana said, stopping us on the sidewalk. "I love you, Eli. You are the most beautiful man I've ever known."

Raul and Esmee had brought out some need in the both of us to reaffirm.

I hardly noticed at the time but now I realized Liana was changing. The way she dressed, the way she ate, the people she had drinks with after class. They seemed to have nothing to do with us, but somehow they did. The changes took her further away from me. Even in bed, the rhythm and intensity had shifted.

The summer before she died, when we returned from the Alps, the semester had started, and then something. What? It was small. A tiff we had. On our trip, we had said "nothing real" to one another. That was what she told me.

No doubt meaningful conversations had become Philippe's department.

I felt the choking feeling, the urge to let tears have their way with me. How would I ever understand what happened?

She betrayed me. Yet, at the same time, she built a monument to our love — two trees twisted together as one, with a song made from her own sacred words.

How could she have done both?

I needed to remember everything about the fall of 1951 to understand. Was I too drunk to look through Liana's boxes again? Was there anything from that fall that might tell me something?

I got up, found myself standing just fine, and went to Zelie's room. I didn't bother bringing them out to the living room. I just tipped the boxes out on Zelie's unmade bed. I didn't think she'd mind. I tossed anything with the date 1951 out toward the hallway, but most of it just sailed wildly around the room.

Until I came to the PNU rally flier. September 15, 1951. The orange sheet was like a flare in a sea of white paper. It was a platform rally, a dozen politicians running for the Conseil de Paris. This was it. *Maybe*. It could have been *here* that she recognized someone. Someone she knew had to face justice. A realization that would lead to her death.

I needed to get out of the apartment. On the sidewalk I walked up to the avenue and caught a cab. I looked at my watch, almost 11:00. I told the cabby, Le Coq Gaulois.

I took the long stairwell down into the club. The place was already in full swing, and the air was heavy with smoke and perfumed sweat.

I got Pierre's attention and he came over pouring a glass. "I'm looking for Zelie."

"So am I," he said with an angry tilt to his head. "She never showed and if she's not here tomorrow she'll be out of a job."

I nodded at him and took a look in the private rooms beyond the bar. A short brunette was heading toward the exit.

"Have you seen Zelie?" I asked.

She shook her head and bit a worried lip.

Outside I stood on the sidewalk a minute and then hailed another cab. Had Yannick grabbed her?

Lamarck and Damremont, I told him. I got in the back seat feeling hot again. My left fist was tight and wanting to inflict pain. I checked my Colt and tried to picture the layout of the Delage's apartment. I'd get her back if they had her.

I paid off the cabby a block early. As I approached I could see an old woman sitting on the front step smoking a cigarette.

"They're gone, Monsieur l'agent," she said, recognizing me.

"Do you know where?"

She just shook her head. "Two nights ago I heard fighting. I watched them from the window load bags into a car and drive off. If you find them, they owe a month's rent."

"And the daughter, she went too?"

"Yes, monsieur, all of them."

I was too dazed to thank her. I just nodded and walked away. I walked a mile before I could think straight again. They had taken Zelie and moved out. Why? Because they suspected her of helping me? Did this mean they were somehow involved in Liana's death? Or was this just some family matter?

If it had to do with our investigation, I needed to consider what Zelie might be forced to reveal. That I was tracking Osval and Liana's killer wasn't news, but if she told them JP was trying to infiltrate the PNU goon squad or that I was looking for Remy Meyette that could be dangerous.

When I reached my apartment I went straight to her room. I checked the drawers, between the mattress and under the bed for anything she might have been hiding. There was nothing but her crumpled clothes. I poured a whiskey and went out to the balcony. The midnight air seemed to smell like bread or flowers or just not of trash.

I had been trying to think of Zelie's disappearance as just a problem that needed to be fixed, but now my gut roiled with worry as I drank. What would they do to her? Would her own mother allow them to hurt her? Torture her for information? I didn't know. I could only hope their primary intention was keeping her from me.

Damn.

If I had already figured out who was behind Liana's death there wouldn't be any reason to take Zelie away. Why hadn't Liana left a few more fucking clues?

What was I missing?

I'd already figured out that the existence of the photo meant more than we knew. Otherwise, why hide it? Why not put it in a frame and hang it on the wall? She would have known who took it.

"Right?" I said aloud to the city.

Somebody must have given it to her.

Unless… no one had.

*

At dawn, I poured some cold coffee with a shot of whiskey and brought my cigarettes to the table. I was exhausted but going to bed was pointless. I changed my clothes and started walking to Les Halles Market. It was a long shot that Yannick would be back to work, but I needed to check. If he collected debts, like Zelie had said, maybe it was from vendors who'd made a bad bet on football or a horse race. I wore the black newsboy cap Liana had bought for me and pulled it down low. Hopefully I looked like the proletariat she secretly admired.

The streets were quiet, just small trucks making deliveries, until the corner at Rambuteau where the clamor of the market materialized into a mob. I wandered through the stalls with throngs of shoppers bargaining with steely-eyed farmers and fish mongers. The air was a cacophony of prices and haggling. This place was popular with pickpockets, so I kept my jacket buttoned up.

I circled the marketplace again and noticed someone standing on an overturned crate. It wasn't Yannick, but he wore a gray suit and fedora hat and had the look of someone biding his time.

When I stopped in front of him he flicked his butt to the cobblestones and raised his brows.

"I'm looking for Yannick. He owes me five thousand francs," I said.

"Yannick's away. And I don't suggest looking for him."

"When will he be back?"

"That's none of your business, pal."

"Then I want to get a message to Ludo," I said on a hunch.

The man crumpled his paper coffee cup and stepped off the crate.

"You're either stupid or want to get hurt."

"Hey," I said, backing up. "I just want to get paid. I don't care by who."

"Ludo ain't got time to waste on you."

I nodded and backed away. He'd told me everything I needed to know. Yannick was one of Ludo's henchmen. When he turned his attention to lighting another cigarette I twisted around and got back out to the street.

I sat at a café across from Alix's gambling den and waited for her to show. The only other patron was an elderly woman wrapped in a shawl with a black poodle on her lap. I pictured Liana as a student wearing culottes and cork shoes and then as an academic who shaved her legs and wore Christian Dior. But it seemed impossible to imagine her wrinkled and gray, or with a poodle on her lap. When I was old, how strange would it be to think of her forever young?

When the thought got too big and I realized it could be hours before Alix might show for work, I paid the waiter and took a walk around the block to clear my head. I extended the trip by going around the park at the Palais Royal. At the corner of Ste. Anne and Therese, I found myself gazing at café goers, and unexpectedly, Alix and Ludo having espresso. Had they spent the night together? Given the time, it seemed obvious. I felt my temper rise.

I picked up a copy of *Le Monde* at the kiosk and leaned against the railing down to the metro. By the time I reached the sports section they both stood up and kissed each other's cheek. Alix started off in the opposite direction and Ludo toward me.

I tilted the paper down just enough to see him coming. He passed the entrance to the metro and I gave him a half block head start before following.

On Colonel Driant he took a left and then another at the next cross street. I accelerated to a fast walk until we reached rue du Louvre where Ludo slowed his pace. He turned into a café. It was the same place I'd seen him standing with Alix a few weeks ago. I guessed this was where he did business.

I waited ten minutes and then went in. A long glass case of pastries stood between me and an old man cleaning the espresso machine. There was a table in the window and two others against the opposite wall. A thick bald-headed man occupied one of the tables. He sat smoking with nothing but an ashtray in front of him.

I ordered a double espresso and then wandered to the back. An arch in the wall led to another room with two long tables and a dozen empty chairs. I noticed a closed door on the other side.

I returned to the counter and waited for my drink. The old man came around the case and pulled out a chair for me at the table near the window. I sat down and looked out on the sunny street with growing apprehension.

A door closed in the back room and a half minute later Ludo and a thug that might have been the twin brother of the smoker at the other table came through the archway. Ludo went to the counter and told the old man to make him whatever "Monsieur Cole" was having.

I shook my head. Of course, everyone in Paris knew who I was.

One of the twin no-necks sat next to me and the other flipped the sign to "Ferme" on the door.

Ludo brought over two espressos and pushed one across the table like any hospitable host.

"This must be just coincidence," he said. "Because I'm sure I've done nothing to interest the spies over at the American Embassy."

"As you say," I answered. "I just needed coffee."

Ludo ignored me and took a sip from his espresso.

"These beans are hard to come by. Luckily, I have many connections, including ones with your CIA. Somewhere I even have a letter of commendation from General Bradley."

"That was then," I said, unimpressed.

Ludo smiled. "That is now. Your war with the communists? I'm on the front line. Ask your boss."

I'd lost interest in my espresso but took a sip anyway.

"You can rest easy," I said, feigning disinterest in his arrangement. "I'm just looking for a missing girl."

Ludo looked over at his man with mock concern.

"Name's Zelie," I continued. "Your goon Yannick has her."

Ludo shot air out his nostrils and shook his head. "She is a beauty, can't blame you there. But she's not missing, not at all. Just has new living arrangements."

I nodded, trying to keep my cool. "Still, I'd like to make sure."

"Rest easy," he said, full of charm. "I'll see to it she's well taken care of — even give her a nice new job."

He smirked at both goons.

I started to get up but baldy held my arm to the table.

"I knew a fella'," Ludo started, "whose girl got picked

up by the Gestapo. Damn fool wanted to break her out. I told him she was already dead. Dead as soon as they nabbed her. But he couldn't let it go, got careless. They killed her right in front of his eyes. Then they tortured him until he gave up the rest of us. We know because they let him go. I had to put a bullet in the back of his head myself."

"Good friend," I said.

"You're right. If he'd listened to me, he'd still be alive." His eyes went cold. "So, take my advice, stay out of my business. It'll extend your life."

I was getting tired of our conversation. "I appreciate all your help," I answered.

The smile was back on Ludo's big face. "Well," he said getting up, "we've got business to attend to. Stay safe."

The bulldozer let go of me and followed his boss.

"Thanks for the espresso," I called after them.

The other thug went back to his dead cigarette in the ashtray.

At the café across the street I ordered a Pernod. The place was light on patrons, but the shade from the awning let me watch Ludo's place without being too obvious.

After twenty minutes I decided to give it another drink. This time a scotch and soda. As the waiter disappeared back inside someone I recognized came walking up the street.

Yannick.

I brought the newspaper up to my nose and watched him go into Ludo's café. My patience had paid off. I left some francs on the table in case he didn't stay long. Five minutes later he was back outside and standing on the curb waving for a cab. But something about his routine wasn't convincing. When he stepped off the curb it was right toward me. He reached behind his back.

I tipped over the marble-topped table before his first shot cracked through the window behind me. I pulled my Colt as another bullet broke the table in two and jumped out firing two shots. He dodged and backstepped.

In a gunfight you never retreat.

I took aim and fired, hitting Yannick in the abdomen. He groaned loudly and collapsed.

I trained my gun on the doorway across the street and went over to the wriggling body. Yannick's face was twisted in agony as he held his gut with both hands.

"Where's Zelie?" I demanded. "Tell me and I'll get you help."

I put my hand over his and applied pressure to the wound.

The pain on his face changed to burning hatred.

"Casse-toi!"

I noticed some movement inside Ludo's café.

"Just tell me where she is!" I said, pressing down on his wound.

He screeched and made a desperate grab for his gun. But his hand slung quickly back to his gut. He was losing a lot of blood.

"Go to hell," he said in strangled English.

I considered putting him out of his misery but instead backed away and side stepped down the street. I saw the old man from Ludo's café dart out to Yannick, but he paid no attention to me.

JP had said things might heat up. Guess he was right. Once I took the corner I wasn't sure where to go. Would they come after me? If I went back to my apartment how long until the police showed up, or Ludo? They'd shoot first and buy off the police later. There must have been witnesses. It was clearly self-defense. I'm sure the Embassy could straighten it out.

The Embassy, that was the safest place. The Marines would keep Ludo out, and I couldn't be arrested on American soil.

I got my bearings as I headed south. Alix's gambling parlor was only a couple blocks away. Not the smartest place, but not the first I'd be looked for either. If I was going to find Zelie I'd need Alix's help.

I caught my breath before hitting the buzzer. A slat in the black door slid open and a man looked out.

"Quoi?"

"I have to speak to Alix, it's urgent," I replied.

The slat closed. I heard muffled voices over an intercom. A bear-sized man opened the door.

"First landing," he said.

If I was as big as him I wouldn't have squeezed by.

I climbed the stairs and opened the heavy door on the first floor. The room was brighter than I expected. Electric chandeliers hung from the high ceiling over green felted tables. There were only a few patrons. A dealer in a tuxedo was shuffling his deck at a poker table.

Alix came out from a door that matched the wall. Her eyes told me she wasn't at all happy to see me. She took my arm and brought me to the bar.

"I'm getting the feeling your boss doesn't like me much," I said, leaning against a stool.

She raised an eyebrow. "You do have that effect on people."

I smiled back. "Know a guy named Yannick?"

"No. Should I?"

"He's one of Ludo's henchmen. I just put a bullet in his gut."

Alix hardly blinked.

"Tell me everywhere Ludo hangs his hat and I'll be on my way."

"Give me one good reason," she answered.

"Remember that girl in my apartment? Your boss has her."

Alix glanced over at the poker tables and then pushed open her office door and led me inside.

"Maybe Ludo didn't care for your new living arrangement," she said, sitting on her desk.

"*Maybe*," I said. "But I want her back."

"If I tell you," she said slowly, "and you don't find her, will you leave Ludo alone?"

"If he's clean, you have my word."

Alix moved behind her desk. "She won't be at his place, too many people all the time. But a year ago he bought some giant estate out in Arques-la-Bataille, close to Dieppe."

She scribbled an address on a slip of paper and handed it to me.

"Thank you," I said. The estate Pascal had invited JP to must be Ludo's.

I wanted to say more but turned to leave.

"And," she said, before I got to the door. "He used to take me to an apartment in Pigalle he called his *safe house*."

Her eyes met mine a moment and then looked down.

"Do you know the address?"

"No, but it was the top floor apartment, a big place. Directly across from Cite Opera."

"Thank you, Alix. I mean it."

She just looked away.

Chapter Eleven

IF LUDO'S MEN TRASHED MY APARTMENT there wasn't a thing I could do about it. I couldn't take everything. I grabbed my army duffle, packed some clothes and toiletries and tossed in the photograph of Liana I kept on the nightstand.

On the way to the Embassy I remembered a stupid argument we'd had over the framed picture. Liana hadn't liked it, but I insisted on keeping it. I had brought it to my office years ago so she wouldn't trash it. I dug into my bag and took out the thick wood frame. Liana was looking back at me as she climbed the stairs of some club in Orleans. How could she hate it so much? There was so much excitement and anticipation in her eyes. I had caught her in an unguarded moment of joy.

Did she hate that I saw her in a way she didn't see herself? Maybe I should have just let her toss it all those years ago. It would have been what she wanted.

When the cab turned onto Honoré I put the frame back in my bag. I had to keep her the way she was to me. I couldn't get to know another Liana now, could I? If I tried, I might lose her again.

In the morning I waited for the newspapers to get delivered at the front desk. On page three there was a short bit about a café window being shot out in the Marais in what was thought to be a mugging gone awry. Ludo had managed to cover it up. Which meant I wasn't a wanted man. Not by the police anyways.

At nine I called the city morgue and told them I was investigating a missing person case for the Embassy. But no corpse had turned up with a gunshot wound. Was Yannick buried in the café basement?

I wasn't sure how long I should stay holed up waiting to find out. Maybe if I put on a black béret and *une marinière* I could walk around Paris posing as an onion seller. I could probably grow a decent moustache in about a week.

The only thing that mattered now was getting Zelie clear of this mess. I needed to take a look at Ludo's "safe house."

I looked at the photograph of Liana again. I had instinctively put it back in the same spot on my desk where it used to be. How often had I looked at it back then? Back when I knew she'd be in my bed that night. Not often. It had become part of the chaos on my desk, something I occasionally put important papers under so I'd know where they were. A paperweight.

I picked it up and leaned back in my chair. Now it represented all my clearest memories of her. This Liana, the one I knew. Who absolutely loved me and no one else. Could I rebuild our lives together starting here, from the years when it was just us? They weren't gone, they hadn't disappeared. Maybe someday I'd even be able to see beauty in the year I shared her with somebody else. There were beautiful moments between us even then. Our time together was short. I couldn't just cut away the last year or more of it. What about all the nights we shared, or that trip to St. Moritz. How could I still hold them in my heart?

There were a couple short raps on the door before it cracked open.

"Come in, Bill," I said, putting the picture back. Bill gave me a sympathetic look as I did. He sat down on the other side of the desk and leaned toward the photograph.

"Can I?"

I nodded and Bill turned it around to him.

"She had a way about her, didn't she?"

I nodded, giving him a tight smile.

"I remember your wedding. Or whatever it was you had in Massachusetts."

"Our reenactment."

Bill laughed. "Man, that was a party. Your family was a hoot. We just danced until we could dance no more. I was with that girl from Topeka, remember her? God, she was a Midwestern beauty. I thought for sure we'd get hitched. Your wedding put the bee in my bonnet."

"What happened?"

Bill made a face. "I was a handful right after the war. Too much for her good upbringing to handle. She hadn't counted on my drinking and crazy stunts. It took a few years to pack all that shit away."

"Well," I said, knowing the shit he was talking about. "You met Katherine and things worked out alright."

Bill nodded. "It worked out."

He patted his pockets for cigarettes and found none. I tossed him the pack on my desk and he lit up, taking a couple of deep drags. His gaze went over to the couch where my shirt lay and then back to me.

"Sure there's nothing you want to get off your chest?"

I reached for the pack of cigarettes.

"I'd like to tell you Bill, but it'll put you in a jam. You have your family to think about. And this swamp is just getting deeper."

"We could have caught a bullet every day for two years. I'm not worried about any swamp. I just want to help out if I can."

"I'm not sure there is anything."

He pushed the chair back so he could lean against the back wall. "Spill it."

How'd he know I'd capitulate?

I gave Bill the major details. Liana's search for whoever betrayed her professor to the Gestapo and how looking into it might have gotten her killed. Then the situation with Zelie's kidnapping and the shootout at the OK Corral.

"Christ almighty," Bill said, slapping the desk. "And here I thought you spent your days getting soused." He lit another cigarette and soaked it all in. "What's the game plan for getting Zelie back?"

"There isn't one," I confessed.

"We going to take a looksee at this *safehouse* tonight?"

I started to get a little hot under the collar. This had been a mistake.

"Bill, this guy's a gangster. One of his men already tried to kill me. I don't want *you* to do a damn thing!"

Bill brushed me off with a crooked smile. "Look," he said, moving from the desk to the window. "This is your deal, you call the shots anyway you see 'em. But you got one gunman up there, maybe more. If she's there, you're going to need me."

The ashtray was on the windowsill and Bill put out his butt.

I grabbed my shirt and managed the buttons with the cigarette still in my hand.

"Bill, what the hell will Katherine and the kids do if you get yourself killed? I can't allow it."

"Like I said, that's your call. But this is war, Eli. And we're soldiers. Some things don't change."

Bill left me to think on that and went out the door. I sat back down on the couch and wondered what the fuck to do.

In the afternoon I called JP at the Union. He said there were no rumors floating around about the shootout I'd been in. He had read the same piece in the paper.

"They could be after you too," I said.

"Don't worry, I have a pistol in my tool box."

"You might need a quicker draw," I cracked.

"It's hard to fix a toilette with a MAS revolver in your belt," he chuckled. "Does any of this prove anything?"

"It means Ludo's involved in Zelie's kidnapping and maybe even Liana's death. Why else try to have me killed? But I don't know anything for sure."

For exercise I took a tour of all four floors of the Embassy and even checked in with the captain of the guard on the fourth. I casually asked if the French police had ever tried to arrest someone inside the Embassy.

He frowned and shook his head. "That won't happen."

He let me up on the roof where a half dozen Marines patrolled. Seeing this made me ask the obvious question. Had anyone ever tried breaking in?

He gave me the same answer, but this time with a smile.

By the time I got back down to my office I knew I had to keep Bill out of this mess. If he got killed it would be on my head. I told him over the phone I wasn't going hunting. There was that reception dinner for the prime minister of Belgium. If he wanted to skip it, I'd cover for him.

"Kind of you," he said. "I'll catch up with you tomorrow."

When the party started winding down, I danced with Sylvia, who gave me a peck on the cheek afterwards.

"You old cad," she said, strutting back to her table. For a woman in her sixties she still had the moves.

Who knew self-exile could be so much fun.

After changing into a darker shirt I headed for the front door. Outside, the city lights seemed trapped in a dingy fog.

I ignored the cab outside and walked across to rue D'anjou and waited longer than usual for another cabby to pass by. When we got close to the Cite Opera on rue Blanche I paid him off and got out.

I put my black hat on and helped hold up the wall of a bar across the street from Ludo's building. I lit a cigarette and gazed up. It was typical Parisian apartments, with five floors. *Néoclassique*, was what Liana had told me once. No lights were on upstairs. It was the corner building so I crossed the intersection diagonally and looked again. Two sets of windows in the back of the apartment were lit. I walked back to the bar, looking into the building's foyer as I did. A pair of black shoes crossed one over the other from a nook under the stairs.

One of Ludo's watchdogs?

I followed the exterior back up to the roof and then over to the building next door. That might be the way in.

I scanned down to the entranceway, where I saw Bill in a black trench coat leaning in the doorway and looking at me.

I crossed the street, suppressing the urge to cuss him out.

"I've always wanted to tell a cabby, 'Follow that car!'" He laughed.

He opened his coat a little so I could see the butt of his revolver. And he patted his chest on the other side too. Was he packing two guns?

"Have you even used it since the war?" I asked through clenched teeth.

"I keep it oiled," he said.

A rather fancy looking couple came down the interior stairwell and into the foyer. Bill wrapped an arm around my shoulder and started slurring nonsense.

When the man pushed the door open, Bill said, "Go on Jack, ring the thingy for your buddy. Go on, ring the thingy."

He leaned his substantial weight on me and I stumbled us toward the open door. The lady gave us a disgusted look and I leaned Bill into the corner of the entrance and watched him stick his foot in the closing door. When the couple had turned down the sidewalk we slipped inside.

We were in a high rent part of town, the stairwell was marble and had the dip in the middle from a hundred years of traffic. We followed it up three flights before Bill stopped me.

"And you think you're out of shape," he said, breathing heavily.

"We've got time," I coughed.

We took the next two flights and found the unfinished wood steps up to the roof door. A piece of pipe was leaning against the door jam and Bill used it to block the door from closing. I walked to the edge to take a look over. The fog was thicker up here and I felt mist on my face. Bill hung back near the door and I remembered that he was afraid of heights. Poor bastard.

We crossed over to Ludo's building by climbing over the two elevated ledges. The roof door was in the same place. Bill tried the handle but it was locked and there was no key-hole to pick.

"I had a feeling," he said. Bill took off his coat and tossed it to the ledge. Under his right shoulder was a short crowbar hanging off a rubber belt.

I smiled and shook my head at him.

He took the loop down his arm and handed the bar to me.

I wedged it into the door frame close to the knob and worked it back and forth until it reached the lock. I put all my weight against the bar until the knob bulged outward and finally gave way with a loud crack.

Bill pulled the door open.

"Think anyone heard that?" I asked him.

"We'll find out."

I pulled out my Colt and Bill followed me down the car-peted stairs. We both stood at the bottom and listened.

All we could hear was the muffled sound of a radio.

"Should I knock on the door?" Bill whispered. "And then you bum rush."

"Let me try and pick it. Maybe we can get the draw on them."

Bill nodded. "Give me the crowbar, I'd rather not shoot anyone if I can help it."

143

"Are you sure about this?" I asked, handing it to him.

"Let's just get in there."

I put the tension pick into the key hole and quietly jiggled the rake until the lock pins gave and then twisted. I looked at Bill who nodded before I pushed the door open.

Before us was an empty living room and then directly ahead a hallway that led to a large opening on the right that was pouring light into the hall. Probably the kitchen. Male voices were clear now and so was the football match on the radio. We moved through the room and stood on either side of the entrance to the hall. Two men were arguing in French about the merits of a player.

"Let's check these rooms," I whispered.

Bill tried the first door and found the bathroom. I stuck my head into the room opposite.

Empty.

A few more steps.

Again I twisted the knob. The master bedroom. I didn't like the idea of Ludo showing Alix into this room. It was gaudy; the covers shimmered like gold silk in the light coming in the windows.

I shook my head at Bill who had just checked another room. He shrugged and nodded in the direction of the lit room. There was no getting to the door just past it without being seen. I pointed at Bill to stay put and moved right to the edge of the light. I peeked around the corner slowly.

When I brought my head back behind the wall Bill was staring at me. I held up two fingers.

The one whose back was to me I didn't recognize, but the one who could've seen me just by looking up from his cards was Yannick.

The bastard had lived.

There was only one move. I mimed the best I could to Bill my intention to hold the gun on them while he checked the last door.

He nodded and moved up the hall until he was right behind me.

I took a breath, then felt Bill's hand on my arm. He tapped his ear. The card game had gone silent. It was just the radio now. Instinctively I crouched down and Bill followed. I peeked around the corner again and a bullet cracked off the molding three feet above my head. I fired blindly into the kitchen and pushed Bill backward down the hall.

"Aidez-moi!" a voice yelled.

Zelie.

Bill had his revolver out and got himself into Ludo's bedroom. I got into the bathroom doorway.

We were in a Mexican standoff. Worse. The man downstairs probably heard the shots and would be on his way up.

Zelie was screaming bloody murder and kicking against the door.

"We need to move, Eli."

I didn't want to leave without her but the entrance to the kitchen was too wide. Then the light went off and the hallway went dark.

I heard Bill say, "Shit."

The window at the end of the hall glowed yellow from the street lamp, and without the reflection, I could see the ironwork of the fire escape.

"Bill, get out the door," I hissed.

He took a couple seconds to get up his courage and then charged down the hall. I fired a shot in the direction of the kitchen as I followed and then another when Bill opened the door, making us a couple of silhouettes in the hall light. As we turned the corner a bullet hit the opposite wall.

We heard the tap of shoes growing louder on the marble stairs.

"Back to the roof."

We reached the stairwell just as a head popped up at the last landing. If I waited a second I'd have a clear shot. Instead I pushed Bill up the stairs, keeping the barrel of my Colt pointed at the hall below.

On the roof, Bill headed in the direction of the building next door, but I grabbed his arm.

"I know how to get her."

"We're outgunned!"

"I know, but they won't expect it."

"You're counting on the element of surprise?" he laughed.

"The fire escape. We get Zelie and keep on going down."

Then I saw the slight shudder. It wasn't the bullets worrying Bill, it was the thought of being on the fire escape this high up.

"You get her. I'll hold the door from the other side of the ledges."

"Ok," I said. It made good sense.

Bill took a breath. "I'll give you a few minutes from when the shooting starts. Then I'll close that door and meet you downstairs."

Bill was already climbing over the exterior walls where he'd left his coat earlier.

I ran across the roof to the far end, peered over, and saw the iron landing about ten feet below. I hefted myself over the side and dangled over the landing. My fingers burned as

I held tight to the edge of the building. Then, when I heard Bill's .45, I let go.

I was now facing the window at the end of Ludo's hallway. The kitchen light was back on and I didn't see any movement inside. There was no point in trying to be quiet now. I kicked in the plate glass window with my boot and smashed some of the sharp teeth holding on at the edges.

I climbed through and pulled out my gun.

"Zelie!"

"Yes! I'm here!"

"Get away from the door!" I said, backing into the kitchen as far as I could go. I rushed at the door and slammed into it with my shoulder. It cracked and swung open. Zelie grabbed me, pulled me up off the floor and then engulfed me in her arms. She sobbed into my chest.

I pulled her off more roughly than I intended and gave her a little shake.

"We need to get out of here. Understand?"

She nodded and wiped her face.

"Out the hall window," I directed. "Don't stop until you get to the street."

She didn't pause a second. I followed, keeping an eye on the front door as I went. Another volley of shots came from the roof.

Come on, Bill. Get out of there.

I barely saw the steps ahead of me and prayed none of them were out.

At the bottom, we swung the ladder down to the alley. I held Zelie by the arm and kept her behind me as we approached the main street. To meet Bill we'd have to go right past the entrance to the building. Had they been smart enough to send a man down?

"Just stay with me," I instructed.

She took my hand with both of hers. I double timed it to the entranceway and took a quick look inside. Nobody.

We ran to the entrance of the next building and stood on the stairs. A half-minute went by before Bill turned the corner of the stairwell and came bolting toward us. He pushed the door open and didn't stop. He was sweating like a boxer. I pulled Zelie down the steps. At the first corner we turned left and kept up the breakneck pace until a cabby pulled up behind us and we all squished into the backseat.

"American Embassy," I said.

The cab pulled away from the curb and I turned to look out the back window the best I could. Nobody had followed us. We were all breathing so heavily the cabby discreetly rolled down his window.

Bill started laughing and suddenly we all were. Laughing like we'd just beat the devil.

For now, we had.

Chapter Twelve

ZELIE DROPPED ONTO THE COUCH as soon as we locked ourselves into my office. I covered her with a blanket and she was asleep within minutes. Guess any catching up on what had happened to her would have to wait until morning. I set two chairs facing each other and put my feet up.

The cabby had let Bill out near Fauchon's so he could collect his nerves before going home. I guessed he needed a drink. He'd tried not to shoot anyone he said. Which meant Yannick, maybe two other gunmen, Ludo, and God knew who else would be looking for us.

That I needed to get us out of town was the understatement of the year. Especially Zelie. She'd asked to help but now I had to keep her safe. Would my parents take her in? How could I convince her to get on a ship to America?

The adrenaline rush was over and all the unanswered questions swirling in my head made me dizzy. Maybe I'd even be able to sleep in these chairs.

It was barely dawn when the pain in my neck got me sitting up, and after rubbing some feeling into my shoulders and arms I went to the window. There was a streak of dark pink across the morning sky. What if this was my last sunrise? The eventuality of darkness for all time seemed distant despite the war and Liana's death. Maybe it wasn't something we could really grasp, no matter how close it came. Or maybe when it was time I'd get it. Maybe all the sunrises I'd seen would flood my consciousness and carry me away.

I gave the pink sky another moment and then turned to Zelie. It didn't look like she'd moved a muscle since lying down last night. What was I going to do with her? I sat on the floor and put my head back against the couch.

I got another hour of sleep before Zelie woke up needing the bathroom. I led her down the hall to the commode.

I left her there and went up to the cafeteria, took a carafe of coffee, two mugs, and a couple of powdered donuts back down to my office. Zelie was sitting behind my desk with the picture of Liana in her hand. It was a popular photograph.

"I like her smile."

"So did I," I said, putting the coffee and donuts down on the desk. I poured two cups.

Zelie put the photo down. "I need a cigarette."

"Top drawer," I said.

Zelie opened it and pulled out a pack of Lucky Strikes.

"You should quit now," I said. "This is what it does to you." Zelie laughed. I lit her cigarette and then my own. "Are you ready to tell me what happened?"

She nodded, pulled one of the mugs closer and blew over the top. "I met him."

"Met who?"

"The Resistance fighter you asked me to find, Remy Meyette."

I coughed up smoke. "You found him!"

"He found me. The first thing I did was go back to that address you gave me. I told the landlady I was trying to find

Remy. That I needed his help to solve the murder of my sister."

"Your sister?"

"If I said I wanted to know who murdered my asshole step-dad, she probably wouldn't have bothered."

"Fair," I said.

Zelie dunked one of the donuts in her coffee and took an oversized bite.

"I told her where I worked," she said with her mouth full. "Two nights later a man tells Pierre he's looking for private time with me. He didn't have money for champagne so I met him at the bar and he told me who he was." Zelie drank some more coffee. "Is this how Americans eat breakfast?"

"Only the fat ones."

"I like it," she said.

"Then what," I prompted.

"He asked me a bunch of questions and I just told him straight. That I was helping you find out what happened to your wife."

"Did he tell you anything?"

"He said he'd find you. But he hasn't?"

"Not yet," I answered.

"Then after my shift I started walking home. A car pulled up and Yannick and two baldheaded goons got out. Yannick was all sick looking and talked like he'd been punched in the stomach. He said my mother wanted to see me. I didn't believe him but they had me cornered. We packed some stuff from the apartment and then they locked me in that room."

"Did they hurt you?"

"After they sent my mother away to find a new apartment Ludo would come in with his little horse crop. He asked about you, what you knew, who was helping you, and about Remy."

"They knew Remy?"

"They wanted to know where he was. I told them about finding his mother, but I gave them the wrong address."

"You did good," I said.

"Ludo said he was going to kill you, Eli. He said I was going to start working for him. *Taking care* of special clients."

"Ludo's not going to hurt you, I promise." I went over to the window and looked out. "Let's hope Remy hasn't gone back into hiding."

"I'm sorry."

"I'm the one who should be sorry, getting you involved in all this."

"I want to be involved. And I want to do more."

"Zelie..."

I let it go. I didn't know what to do next. But there was something we needed to talk about. "Look, I don't blame you for anything you may have told Ludo. You've been very brave. But I need to know everything, all of it."

Her eyes dropped to the floor.

I sat back down and put my hand on hers. "It's okay."

"I thought if I told him most of it I could keep a couple things to myself, but it was like he already knew all the answers. He'd smack my legs before I could even say anything. He knew your father-in-law was helping you. And that woman Alix."

"He said that?"

"And he asked me what you knew about Marc."

"Who's Marc?"

Zelie shrugged. "I said I didn't know. I only told him you wanted to know who killed your wife. And that you thought Remy could help."

"Did he give a last name to this Marc?"

Zelie shook her head. "Who do you think he is?"

"I don't know. But I don't think they figured you'd have the chance to share his name with me. I bet our friend Remy knows."

"We can go to the landlady today."

"As soon as we walk out these gates we might be shot. We need to lay low. I'll send a messenger. But you can't stay here another night. If you do, I'll have the First Secretary down here asking questions. But..." I said, suddenly knowing just where she could go. "I know a place in the countryside where you'll be comfortable until this is over."

The sad, shame-faced girl went rigid and stood up. "I don't want to hide somewhere until this is over. I want to bring that bastard Ludo down."

"Zelie, I need you to stay alive. Do you understand that? People are going to start dying now. Maybe me, maybe JP, Alix, you..." I knew the list went on.

"I don't care," she said. She sat on the couch and I saw her lips quiver.

"Look, if Remy will meet me, you can come. He seems to trust you."

She didn't acknowledge what I said, but the sniffling stopped.

"I'm going upstairs to send a messenger. You just rest."

Zelie got up and wrapped her arms around me. I let my cheek sink to the top of her head. She was warm like a stove.

153

"I'll see you soon," I said, letting her go, and went to the door.

"Don't do anything without me," she said.

"I won't."

At noon I brought Zelie upstairs to the cafeteria and she ate a hamburger and fries like a starving animal. Even ten years later the French were struggling to feed their population. I went up to the counter and brought back two pieces of chocolate cake.

She melted when she took her first bite.

"You could eat like this every day in America."

She gave me a quizzical look. "Is that an invitation?"

"It is. But I want you to go now, today even. You can stay with my parents when you arrive," I said.

She looked toward the buffet and didn't answer.

"What's here for you? Why not start over in a growing country?" I prodded.

"Will you? Will you go too?"

"I might, when this is over."

"Then ask me again," she said.

It was a pleasant thought that we might get out of this mess alive. Before the feeling grew, I stamped it out in my mind. Right now, hope was dangerous. It would make me careful and then I'd make a mistake.

"Let's get back down to the office."

Zelie wrapped the rest of her cake in a napkin and we left the plates on the long wood table.

The phone was ringing when we got downstairs and I unlocked my door quickly enough to pick up. It was the messenger.

"I delivered your note to the landlady," he said. "Then she asked me to wait. After a minute a man came into the room and wanted me to bring him to see you. But the front desk won't let me go any further, you'll have to come up."

I slammed the phone down and grabbed Zelie by the hand. We both ran down the hall and up the stairs. At the front desk, Zelie and Remy recognized each other and we led him back down to my office.

"Cigarette?" I offered.

He looked at me like a man about to be condemned to the noose.

"Okay, why not."

I handed him the pack and he moved to the windowsill to use the matchbook sitting there. Zelie perched on the edge of the couch.

Remy gave the pack a couple of perfunctory hits against his palm and then pulled a cigarette out. We both watched him light it like he was about to perform a miracle.

"In the spring of '52," he started. "I was an administrator for SNCF. On my way home from work one day a woman approached me and introduced herself. She seemed unsure of what to say next, but there was also something very determined about her. Like she had set herself on a course and was going to follow it."

He drew on his cigarette and then continued. "At that time I had no reason to deny my identity. When she asked if I'd been in the Resistance in Paris I admitted it. She asked me some questions about Gael Favret, a professor of hers who'd been taken by the Gestapo. But I didn't know anything about him. I was not part of any particular network then. Instead, I coordinated between various contacts and

155

a few well-placed French officials who believed eventually the Allies would win. It was some of these administrators who misplaced transfers for art and antiques, and who also, sometimes, when they thought they could get away with it, passed intelligence from their departments.

"Your wife explained," he went on, "that while collecting information on PNU candidates for the Communists, she recognized a man she knew during the war. His name was Gustave Dubroc. But when inquiring after him, she was told his name was Marc Bechard."

"Marc!" Zelie blurted.

"She told me," Remy continued, "during the war she did secretarial work for him. He was an administrator at the Sorbonne. After liberation he disappeared. She thought maybe he'd gotten himself killed. While cleaning out his things she found a photograph of Gael under the desk. She suspected Gustave may have had something to do with her professor's death. The Resistance network Gael was a member of was brought down by the Gestapo in the winter of 1942."

"Do you know how it happened?" I asked.

"We tried to understand how networks were taken down. But there were so many ways to be betrayed. An informant, someone brutally interrogated and then turned to save their neck or their family's. We did not know there were any survivors from that network. Gustave may have even been part of it. I don't know. But, when she asked me to help her find evidence that this man was a traitor I thought of someone who might be able to help. He was one of those latecomers to the cause, who joined the Resistance after everyone knew which way the wind was blowing. But he was brash, took extraordinary risks, and got results. I kept track of him after the war. He had gotten into the black market and had expanded into other vice trades. He seemed like the best man to find out if there was dirt on this Gustave."

"Ludo Orban," I said.

"Yes, Ludo. Not only did he find dirt, he came up with an entire Gestapo file on him. He showed it to me briefly. Gustave was a scumbag, trading on the lives of his fellow countrymen. But Ludo wouldn't give me the file, he wanted a ransom for it. I told Liana but she had no way of paying the kind of money he was asking. On the same day Liana was killed, I came home to find a gunman in my living room. If he hadn't been so careless as to smoke a Gitanes while he waited to kill me, I too would be dead. I called the Sorbonne to warn her, but they couldn't find her. I'm sorry I did not inform you of what really happened. I didn't even know she had a husband. I left Paris and got a job in Marseille under another name. I'd adjusted to my new situation in life when I heard from my mother. I went to talk to Zelie at Le Coq. When I left, I recognized one of Ludo's men in a car outside. I didn't know if he knew who I was or not. Or if Zelie was part of some trap. But he didn't follow, so I just went back to my hotel."

"He did recognize you," I informed him. "When they kidnapped Zelie later that night they asked her about you."

Remy looked alarmed. "It could mean that Yannick didn't intend to kidnap Zelie that night, but when he recognized me leaving the club he decided she had to be taken out of the equation. They didn't know if I'd told her anything."

I stood and went over to the window. How could I have been so oblivious?

"Once Ludo realized what kind of influence he'd have

by blackmailing Gustave with his Gestapo file," Remy continued, "a sitting councilor of Paris, with aspirations of becoming prefect — he didn't want anyone ruining it. We were liabilities, your wife and I."

I leaned against the wall, stunned.

"But they killed a PNU goon," I said when I could think straight. "Osval, the man found next to Liana."

Remy shook his head. "Maybe they sent him to rough her up, and then used his death to deflect suspicion from themselves."

It all seemed so incredible.

"Where did he get the Gestapo file?" I asked, ignoring the leaden feeling in my gut.

Remy shrugged. "I only know that they exist. The government pretends they don't have them. They're too embarrassed. When Ludo put the squeeze on Gustave, he must have asked him who might have put me on his trail. The answer, of course, was your wife. It is likely he also recognized Liana at the rally."

"He condemned her."

"That is my guess."

I wanted to explode.

"But you must do nothing to him. If you were to kill a government councilor it would practically be an act of war. It might incite international hostilities."

Could there be any other resolution than the death of those responsible? Maybe Gustave had not pulled the trigger, or even recommended that Ludo kill Liana. But he had caused Gael's death and consequently her own as she sought justice for him. The same justice I intended to fulfill. But there might be another way. We needed the file Ludo had on him.

"I have," Remy said, putting out his cigarette, "always felt responsible for your wife's death. I should not have trusted someone as ambitious and reckless as Ludo. I am truly sorry. It has weighed heavily on me these years."

Zelie gave me an expectant look. Remy seemed on the verge of weeping.

I put my hand on his slouched shoulder.

"I needed to know. Thank you. And what happened was not your fault."

We stood that way for a few more moments, Remy's head bowed from shame.

"Did Liana ever tell you what she intended to do with the proof of Gustave's collaboration?" I asked.

"The only subsequent time we met she told me she wanted to ruin Gustave's career. The file would have accomplished that, I assure you."

I went back behind my desk and picked up the phone. I tried Alix's home number first, then called JP at his Union.

"Can you meet us somewhere?" I asked him. "I want to take Zelie to your nephew's."

"Outside Brasserie Lipp in 30 minutes."

I hung up and looked over at Zelie. Her look was more resigned than angry.

"What will you do?" Remy asked.

"Make them pay," I answered. "All of them."

"I am with you," he said. "I need to be."

"There's a place in the country we can hash this out. But we need to get out of here unnoticed. Did you see anyone when you came in with the messenger?"

"Just the cabs out front. But one of them could easily be an informant for Ludo."

I knew what I needed to do, but it would be my last favor. I dialed the phone again and Sylvia answered.

"Is the First Secretary in?" I asked her.

"I'll put you through, Eli."

When he picked up it took me a couple beats to get the words out of my mouth.

"You want to borrow the ambassador's car and driver?" he laughed.

"On account of the informant in my office," I said. "He was seen coming in, so I have to get him out behind tinted windows or he's a goner."

"Well, in that case. But what's this to do with showing Bill the ropes?"

Before I could answer he laughed again. "Never mind. We got an interesting cable from Washington today."

"Really?" I asked, feigning surprise. "Who from?"

"The CIA wants you on a plane *tonight*. I had to remind them we don't take orders from them. But they do have a way of getting what they want, eventually."

Ludo had sicked the agency on me.

"They give me the creeps, the lot of them," the First Secretary said, breaking the silence. "As for the car — I'll let the chauffer know the score."

"Thank you, Robert."

"Good luck." The phone clicked.

"We need to go," I said.

From behind the dark windows of the ambassador's black Chrysler I looked out at the cabs and pedestrians. A man leaning against a tree in the park looked up from his paper as we passed by and then turned the page.

JP was waiting just where he said. We parked around the corner and then piled into the van. Zelie sat up front, squeezed between JP and Remy. I sat on a tool box in the back.

I only told JP when I introduced Remy that he had been helping Liana track down Gael's killer. The details, how he may have inadvertently got Liana killed, could wait.

It was a long ride out to Burgundy and I clanged around in the back of the van while trying to listen to what was being said up front. Three things were established while I held onto rubber tubing dangling from the van's ceiling. The first was that Ludo needed to die. The second was that before he did so he needed to reveal where the Gestapo file was. And the third thing we determined was that accomplishing the first two things would be very difficult. When there was gravel under the tires we finally stopped, and I eagerly jumped out the back.

Henri greeted us and gave Zelie a suspicious look. "Another prisoner?"

"Yes," she said, giving me a dirty look.

"Well, you're welcome here," he said, laughing.

We followed Henri inside.

"And what about Alix?" JP asked, pulling me aside. "Is she with us or Ludo?"

"With us," I said. "Once she knows the truth."

"Let's hope," he said.

"Ludo thought Alix was helping Eli," Zelie said. "But maybe he was trying to fool me, to see what I'd say."

"It doesn't matter," JP said bitterly. "If she tried leading Ludo into a trap, he'd smell it a mile away."

Henri brought out percolated coffee and brandy and then went back to the kitchen.

"There must be some way to trick him into retrieving the file," Remy said, pouring coffee.

"What if he needed to use it," Zelie said. "It's blackmail, right? What if he thinks Marc, I mean Gustave, isn't in his pocket anymore?"

JP started to say something but then stopped and smirked. "Get me in the same room with Gustave and I'll convince him Ludo doesn't have his file anymore. I'll say I saw it get burned or something."

Remy nodded. "He might believe you. He'd want to. But if not, you might be arrested for holding a city councilor hostage."

JP shrugged.

"Ludo will need to prove to Gustave he still has his file," I said. "When he does we ambush him and take it."

Remy got up and added brandy to his coffee.

"When JP meets with Gustave," he said, taking a sip, "what if JP tells him he represents a rival gang of Ludo's? And he happens to know that Ludo's safe house was broken into and his Gestapo file stolen."

"And you're renegotiating the blackmail," I said when I caught on.

"He'd want proof," JP said.

"Maybe. Or maybe not," Remy answered.

"You saw the file," I said to Remy. "Could we recreate it?"

"I flipped through it. There were maybe twenty pages of

carbon papers. A dozen photographs stapled to some. I do remember the top sheet. It was a form I'd seen before, a Gestapo personnel sheet. There was a passport sized photo of Gustave."

"No matter how good a forger we find it wouldn't pass more than a brief glance," JP said.

There was a pause in the debate. JP poured himself a brandy and Zelie held her glass out to him. He looked at me and I gave a nod. He poured her a couple fingers.

"Couldn't there have been a fire?" I said, mesmerized by the candle on the table. "We recreate the folder and part of the top sheet. But the rest of the papers and photographs are charred. The bluff only needs to work a short time."

"I know a man who did this kind of work during the war," Remy replied. "I can find him."

"I'll tell Gustave we had hoped to take over blackmailing him," JP said. "But since the file was destroyed all we require of him is to end his relationship with Ludo."

"He should be happy to comply," Remy concluded.

"Ludo will deny it's destroyed," JP went on. "And having just seen the burnt file Gustave will insist Ludo prove it still exists."

"That's when we get it."

Jean-Paul nodded. "It could work."

"It will," Zelie said excitedly, finishing her drink.

"I like this girl," JP said.

"Except," I said, glancing her way, "when we get to America, the drinking age is 21."

She smiled sweetly, "Of course, uncle."

I shook my head at her.

"Then our next move is recon," said Remy. "We need to

know the movements of Gustave and we need to know where Ludo is keeping himself and what his defenses are."

"I'll take Gustave," JP said.

I told Remy I could tail Ludo.

He nodded. "I'll get reacquainted with my old friend the forger."

"Zelie, you need to stay here," I said. "I'll show you how to use the shotgun. Your duty is to defend our base."

She nodded with her chin up.

"Then let's get a good night's sleep," JP said. He headed for the door.

I knew he was going to find Henri. What we were preparing wasn't fair to him. But this was the only safe place we could meet. My mind turned back to Alix. Was she safe? Would she agree to come out here for a while? It was worth asking.

I stood outside on the porch a minute and looked over the dusky farmyard. It wasn't that long ago I had that unusual conversation with Mia. I wondered how she was doing back with that pissant Philippe. Would everything be back to normal between them? Or would what happened eat away at their relationship? I wanted Philippe to suffer, but I did not want the same for her. There probably was no way to have one without the other.

The screen door swung open. Zelie stood beside me with a double-barreled shotgun in her arms.

"No time like the present," she said.

"Let's go behind the barn."

There was a wooded area about a dozen yards beyond the mowed lawn. A bale of hay left to rot against the pasture

THE GLASS TREE

fence would serve as a target. I dragged it over to the woods and came back to Zelie.

She handed me the shotgun and I pushed the release latch to break it open. The barrels were empty.

"Here are the shells," she said, pulling them out from her pant pockets. "Henri said there was a whole box."

I took the green cased shells and showed her how they fit into the barrels and how the gun latched back together.

"This is going to have a good kick," I said. "Just hold it beside your hip. You don't need to be a marksman. The shell is full of lead pellets that spray out like angry hornets."

I held the gun just how I told her and pointed it at the bale of hay. "So, just aim in the right direction and pull the first trigger."

The right barrel exploded fire and smoke. The bale of hay tumbled back. I ran over to the hay bale and pushed it up again.

Then I broke open the gun and said, "You still have one more barrel loaded. All you have to do is latch it back together, aim, and pull the inside trigger."

She took the gun tentatively, put her left hand on the fore-end and hugged the gun against her mid-section. Then after a deep breath, moved her pointer finger to the trigger and swung the barrels toward the hay bale.

The recoil knocked her over.

She laughed and sat up. "Look."

"A bull's-eye," I said.

I held out my hand and she pulled herself up. I grabbed the shotgun and we walked back to the house.

"Eli," she said, still holding my hand. "If you get killed, I'll be on my own. I'll become just what we both know I will." She leaned up for a hug and kissed my cheek. "I love you, Eli."

"I love you, Zelie."

She held me tight and then let go. She ran into the house so I wouldn't see her tears. I felt my own eyes water and used my sleeve to dry them before I followed her inside.

I supposed I did love Zelie. In a way I'd never given much thought: paternally. Liana had never gotten pregnant. I always thought she was kind of relieved not to be a mother. The kind of love we had for each other, that impossible kind of love, had died with her. I knew it deep down.

If I lived through what was coming, and Zelie agreed to a future in America, maybe I could at least make things right for her. Set her on a course headed far away from places like Le Coq Gaulois.

Maybe I'd find an old house somewhere in the country and lead a perfectly quiet, pleasant life. More than I could hope for alone in Paris. But I didn't get to start over. I might escape the city that reminded me every day of Liana. But whatever I might also lose or someday regain, love for another woman would never be one of them.

Chapter Thirteen

IN THE MORNING JP KNOCKED ON MY DOOR. I got up and went downstairs where Cosette had prepared eggs and ham. For someone whose house had been appropriated by a mad uncle-in-law she was very accommodating. We left after that. Remy got out at the metro station at Père Lachaise and then JP left me in the thirteenth arrondissement where I could get a cheap hotel room.

"Take these," he said, handing me a small pair of binoculars. "Might be best if you don't get too close to Ludo."

"Thanks," I said. "Where are you staying?"

"There's an unoccupied building we're working on. If a co-worker sees me there it won't raise alarms. I'll see you in a couple days."

"Good luck."

He nodded and drove off.

The first thing I had to do was find Alix. I took a cab over to her apartment and rang her bell. There was no reply.

I walked over to the gambling den, but this time sent a kid with a message for her. He came back to the corner a minute later. The big man at the door had told him she wasn't there.

He handed me back the note. I gave him 200 francs and asked if he'd like to triple it. He nodded hungrily.

I hailed a cab and we took it over to the Royal Jardin. We got out at the corner of the park and walked to rue du Louvre.

"I need you to go into that café over there and order an espresso to go," I said, handing him a 100 franc note.

He nodded, but his face said he thought I was crazy.

"While you're in there," I said, "I want you to look around for a big man in a suit, slick black hair and a ruddy face. Try and look in the back room without being seen."

The boy nodded again, this time with a spark in his eye. A little spy in the making. He ran down the street and into the Etalon Blanc.

After a couple minutes I started to get nervous. Had they made him for a snitch? I spent another minute tapping my foot and then saw the kid walking back to me with a paper cup in his hand.

"What did you see?" I asked, taking the cup from him.

"The man wasn't there. Just some old guys having coffee. No one was in the back room."

"Okay, you did good." I gave him the 600 francs I promised and extra for the metro.

"Thanks, Yank," he said.

The kid was sharp. I thought my American accent was long gone.

I walked back down to the park. I took the precaution of wearing my old fedora hat and my government-issued sunglasses. At the very least someone would have to double take to recognize me.

As I walked through the park I wondered how many of these tourists enjoying the spring weather were also tracking down the man they intended to kill.

Maybe I wasn't the only one, I thought wryly.

I didn't know where Ludo's apartment was so decided to stake out the "safe house" instead. It seemed just as likely he'd be there as anywhere. I sat in the bar across the street and read the paper. Apparently the Geneva Conference was sending French forces to South Vietnam. I hoped we didn't get involved in that mess. After two hours of clacking billiard balls I saw a black sedan pull up to Ludo's building. Then another. Two men got out and gathered around the entrance to the lobby. Another minute and Ludo came out the front door. He hung around with the men; one of them lit his cigar. Maybe he didn't want them to think he was worried about getting shot. Then the group broke up and Ludo got into the back seat of the second sedan.

Unless I managed to get a cab in the next thirty seconds I was going to lose them. I dropped some bills on the zinc table and navigated my way out to the sidewalk as the two sedans made a right at the intersection.

There were no cabs, so I hoofed it to the corner. The cars were already out of sight.

"Thought I might find you here," someone said behind me.

I turned to find the silver haired CIA officer I'd talked to about Liana's murder. His theory was the same as the French SDECE: that it had been Russian agents.

"I didn't know you were looking for me," I answered, not recalling his name. "You could just come by the Embassy."

"Nothing official, son," he said with a disarming smile. "Just a friendly chat."

He put his hand on my back and led me around the corner.

"Let me guess," I said. "This is about Ludo Orban."

He gave me a pat. "He's important to us, Eli. Why are you suddenly giving him a hard time?"

"Because," I said. "He killed my wife."

The man stopped in his tracks. "I remember you asking about that. I thought we figured it for the Russians."

"Well, I figured it different."

"How so?"

I didn't know if he was bullshitting me but I played along.

"She was about to expose a politician in Ludo's pocket as a Nazi collaborator. He didn't like that."

"Was he a collaborator?"

"Ludo has his Gestapo file, that's how he's running him."

"We don't know all the details," the agent said, starting to walk again. "Only that this Ludo fellow has more than one politician under his thumb and is willing to play ball with the United States government."

"We get into bed with gangsters?" I said.

"Anyone but the communists," he answered. "You do remember what our job here is, don't you?"

"I'll admit I forget sometimes," I replied.

"Have any proof he's done what you say?"

"I'm working on it."

"I doubt Washington will care either way. They'll say it's for the 'greater good' to keep our relationship with Ludo. But personally, I'm with you on this."

"Can you give me a little more time?" I hedged.

"I might have a hard time finding you for 48 hours," he answered. "But if you keep messing with Ludo, they're going to want you on a plane and they'll ask me to put you there."

"Understood," I said.

"Don't make a mess, Eli."

With that he turned and walked back toward the corner. I kept on up the street and after a minute a hopeful cabby pulled over.

It was worth seeing if Ludo's crew were at the café. I paid the fare at the corner and walked a block. Two sedans parked out front. My disguise not withstanding I decided to skip a drink at the place across the way where the window was still boarded up.

Instead I smoked a cigarette at the corner and considered the likelihood that wherever the black sedans were, Ludo would be too. More useful right now would be to find Alix. I went down to the metro. The Vincennes – Pont de Neuilly line took me close enough. I tried Alix's bell and then the other apartments. Nobody buzzed me in or even answered.

Fuck.

I picked the lock in broad daylight. What a moment for a flic to walk by. My shoes seemed abnormally loud as I climbed up to the fourth floor. I gave Alix's door a couple of hard knocks. When she didn't answer I took the lock picks out again.

Her apartment looked the same as it had a week ago. I checked the fridge: a half empty bottle of milk. Her bed was made. Why did that surprise me?

The last room I checked was the bathroom. In any good spy movie a message would be left on the mirror. All I needed to do was run the hot water to get some steam. I used my breath on a few spots. There was no message.

"Where are you, Alix?"

Checking Ludo's apartment or the safe house for her

meant showing my face in places it might get shot off. If I stayed put, maybe, just maybe, Alix would show up.

I lay down on the bed and stretched out. I could smell her seductive perfume on the pillow. It made me sentimental for what might have been.

As I contemplated, I heard the apartment door click open. Alix? But maybe not. I got out of the bed and pulled out my Colt. I just reached the back of the door when it flew open and a man strode quickly over to the closet.

He selected a few dresses, hung them over his arm and then dug around for shoes. He pivoted to the dresser, where he tossed clothing randomly into a sack. I heard him swear. A minute later he was done. I heard his steps down the hall and the door closing.

I hadn't recognized him but he must have been one of Ludo's men. There was no doubt Ludo was keeping her close now. Not allowed to collect clothing for herself, but in need of evening wear. Did they have reservations somewhere tonight?

I waited ten minutes and then left. I could probably find her at one of the addresses she'd given me. But not alone, and I wasn't in the mood for another rescue. She might be a captive, but I guessed she wasn't being made to suffer too much.

I walked back to the corner where I could observe Ludo's café and made note when he and his gang got back in their cars and pulled away. I caught a cab and followed them to what must have been Ludo's apartment.

After an hour I figured they were in for the night. On my way back to the hotel, I detoured into a bar on rue Clisson and stared up at the ceiling, wishing everything that had happened in the past two years hadn't.

What would I do for it to be true? How many times after Liana was killed did I try to wake up from it like a bad dream? I'd escape for a second and then it crashed down on me all over again. It was real and there was no way out.

A half dozen patrons from Paris's downtrodden were congregated at the other end of the tunnel-like bar and giving their attention to the one woman in the group. The cheery gang tried pulling me into their orbit by waving me over but I begged off and sat in the back and watched the bartender. He was a skeleton of a man, but his muscles, bones, sinews somehow worked in unison to pour beers and laugh at jokes.

In the morning I'd confirm Ludo's schedule. Of course, when the day came to set our trap his routine might change. But what could be done? All we could do was hope.

The scumbag was living his last days on earth. It was two years more than he deserved. He'd been on borrowed time since the moment my wife's body went cold on the sidewalk.

That fire in the pit of my stomach still burned. To kill a man. To take away his future, his ambitions, his loves, his morning coffee. Why force me to do it? Why give a man no other option but to murder you?

And why had Liana done the same? Giving us no chance to find another path. One that led to a future together and away from Philippe. Why leave me out of her plans to ruin Gustave? Did she think I wouldn't want to help avenge her friend or whatever Gael had been to her? I felt myself pushing away a feeling I'd had before. *I didn't know my wife.*

173

There it was, sitting on the bar beside my glass of Suze like some grotesque creature.

I picked up my glass and poured everything in it down my throat. But no amount of alcohol could overcome that thought. I wouldn't be able to drink my way out from under it. I needed to trust the voice that told me Liana was the woman I knew her to be. And only partly a woman I didn't.

A fit of laughter from the gang near the door brought me back. Back to a bar for Paris's lost causes.

I ordered another Suze, horrible as it was. I'd end up here if I believed my wife never loved me. A place people went to be forgotten.

Chapter Fourteen

AFTER AN HOUR OF WATCHING LUDO'S PLACE from across the block, two black sedans pulled up. When Ludo came out the door he handed a suitcase to one of his henchman and got in the back seat. A moment later Alix exited the building and joined him. A different hood put two cases in the trunk.

When the cars pulled away from the curb I ran into traffic to stop a cab. When we got close to the edge of the city I realized they were not heading to the airport. This was the way to Arques-la-Bataille. I told the cabby to bring me to the station at Pontoise.

The next train on the Dieppe line was in an hour. Just enough time to run to the nearest shop for a bottle of Armagnac, a snack and double espresso.

The train out into the banlieues was one of the older models. A survivor from the war I guessed. I knew a lot of them met their demise from American-made bombs.

When we reached the countryside I started to relax. Old farm houses surrounded by trees and crooked fields of barley and rapeseed coasted by. What would it be like to live outside of Paris in some ramshackle house? What would it have been like with Liana, if she had never become a professor and we ran a farm instead?

There had been that day trip we took to Clamart early

on. They still had signs up warning of mines in the fields. We'd walked out of town and stopped at a house that looked abandoned. It was small and cozy looking, just the kind of place for newlyweds to start a family. Squared off by stonewalls in the back were scraggly looking fruit trees. It was late spring and buds flowered on most of them. Liana fell in love instantly.

I'd spun for us an imaginary day at this house, where we picked cherries and made pies and raised sheep and chickens and lived like country folk. We held each other tight and wondered for a moment if it could all be true.

Why this fate and not that one?

I almost cracked the seal on the bottle of Armagnac, but I needed to find my way to Ludo's estate tonight. I let the memory of Liana and the farm drift away. There would never be an answer for why I lost her.

I tried to focus on the task at hand. What would Ludo have for keeping away unwelcome guests? Couple of dogs? I added some chuck steak to my shopping list.

After an hour of passing fields, I fell asleep. When I woke up a half hour later, I made my way to the dining car. The thought of steak for the dogs gave me the idea of ordering a rib eye and a Jenlain blonde.

After finishing my second Jenlain, I wrapped the rib eye bone in my napkin and slipped it into my coat pocket.

At Arques-la-Bataille I found a room at the Auberge d'Arques, a rather dull place but with a down bed and pillow. The man behind the desk had a map of town that he let me borrow. I sat in one of the uncomfortable wood chairs in the "lobby" and studied it. I guessed I could hike out to the estate in under an hour. I spent the afternoon at cafés and then back at the inn napped until dusk.

The main road out of town was paved but I had a feeling it would become dirt before long. The evening faded from dusk to dark and I looked upward to see if any stars would be out for my walk home. It was likely to be pitch black. Another thing one forgets when not in the city. I'd be lucky to see the road two feet in front of me.

There had only been one car in the last couple of miles. Its headlights shown against the night so far off in the distance it took nearly five minutes before I needed to duck behind a stone wall. No sense taking any chances being seen. From my crouch I watched as a yellow Colorale passed by with an old man hunched over the wheel. He took so long getting here because he was going about fifteen miles an hour.

I passed two dilapidated farms with coal smoke trickling from the chimneys.

At a long stone drive with stone pillars flanking the entrance I stopped and heard barking in the distance. Some lights twinkled maybe a quarter mile down. This must be the estate.

I took the driveway until I was within a stone's throw of the imposing home. There was no chance of being seen in this inky black. The intermittent yapping of a dog came from inside the house. One problem averted, for now.

This was clearly not one of those old, crumbling estates you hear about, mortgaged to the hilt. The lawn was cut short, landscaped bushes and flowers budded along the edge of the drive. I circled the house to the left, away from the front door and at a distance that my movement would not be noticed.

Only one room downstairs had bright light glaring out the window. The kitchen maybe? A maid cleaning? I closed the distance to the window in a slow-moving crouch and peeked in from the bottom edge.

Two men at a peasant table with a baguette between them. I could tell the one with his back to me was Ludo by his broad shoulders and tan suit. Across from him sat a balding, middle-aged man, with a face that made me think of a weasel. This was probably Pascal.

The dog I'd heard coming up the drive trotted into the room. Pascal patted his head. I lowered to the ground. Dogs had a sixth sense. I gave him a chance to bugger off.

Leaning against the wall I could see one of the second floor rooms light up. I waited for someone to cross the window, but nobody did. I felt a dampness seeping in at the seat of my pants. It was going to be a long walk back to the hotel. I peered back in the window. The dog was gone. Both men stood up and left the room, clicking the light off as they went. The window to my right lit up and I decided, since I couldn't hear what they were saying, to get back to creeping around the rest of the house. I guessed a place like this would have a dozen or more bedrooms. A couple of big living rooms downstairs, an office no doubt, a wine cellar and maybe more than one kitchen.

Was it worth risking a broken window to take a tour inside? But who knew how late these two might be up. Better to set myself up somewhere in the cow field tomorrow and see who came out. That most of the other windows in the estate were dark only meant some people might be asleep.

At the opposite side I saw only two cars, one sedan and

a Talbot Lago. Which meant Ludo did not bring his whole army out here, maybe just himself and a driver. The other car of henchman must have turned around when Ludo was safely out of Paris.

I made my way back around the house, stopping again at the window with the light on. Pascal and Ludo were having a cognac by the fireplace. A gangster and a PNU power broker. How cozy.

The light switched back on in the room with the table. I peeked in the window. Alix was pouring herself a drink.

I tapped as lightly as I could against the windowpane until she looked up. There was the shock I expected and then she pointed toward the back of the house and mouthed the word "kitchen."

I looked in dark windows until I came to what looked like the kitchen. After a moment the window opened. Alix crouched down so her face was framed by the sill.

"What are you doing here?" she hissed.

"Ludo murdered your sister, we have proof. You need to come with me."

"What proof?" she asked.

"I can't explain it all here, but your sister was about to expose a politician for being a traitor during the war. A politician in Ludo's pocket. He had her killed."

"How do you know this?" she asked, looking behind her to the door.

"A reliable source," I said. "Look, Alix, you're a bargaining chip now, protection for Ludo against your father and me."

She looked troubled. "He trusts me, Eli. I know what it looks like, but he won't hurt me. He loves me, I think."

"Alix," I begged.

"He won't hurt me," she repeated. "He won't."

"Then help us," I pressed. "Ludo has been blackmailing this politician with his Gestapo file. If you tell me where his safe is, I'll prove it to you."

"I don't know where it is. His office maybe, but the door is locked."

"Which room is it?"

"Next to the room where they are now. It doesn't have a window."

"Can you get Ludo out of the house tomorrow?" I asked.

"The three of us are riding in the morning, probably around ten."

"Who else is here besides Pascal?"

"Ludo's driver, a couple of house staff."

"Okay," I said. "I'll take a look in his office. Are you sure you want to stay?"

"Maybe you're wrong about all this."

Her hand was on the windowsill and I took it. "Alix, he's going to kill us, or we're going to kill him."

"I believe you," she said. She closed the window without another word and headed toward the door.

When I reached the road I picked up my pace and walked along to the sound of gravel and the rhythmic chirp of crickets. I had an uneasy feeling and didn't know if it was jealousy or the way Alix had reacted to what I'd told her.

I reached town feeling like a frozen piece of leather. Outside the inn, I patted myself down, rubbed my cheeks and fixed my collar before opening the door. But I needn't have worried. The aubergiste was sound asleep behind the desk.

Chapter Fifteen

I SLEPT LIKE THE DEAD. My neighbor, who let his door slam in the morning, woke me just before the alarm clock. I managed to wash up and get down into the street by eight.

At the edge of town, I caught a ride with a farmer heading home from delivering eggs. He dropped me a quarter mile from Ludo's estate and didn't ask any questions. Again, I hopped over the low stonewall running along the road and started into the recently harvested wheat field. I did my best to walk along the drainage ditch, climbed over more stonewalls and continued on into fields that would be hay by fall.

My boots were caked in mud by the time I reached the curtain of trees perched over the pasture that ran down to the estate. The earthy smell would be stuck to me now. Whoever sat next to me on the train back to Paris would think I was a farmhand looking for some Parisian fun.

I got myself next to a wide old oak tree, squatted down against the trunk and took out my binoculars. From here I could see the back of the house and the side facing the barn. I noticed both cars were still in the drive.

Nothing was moving in the rooms facing the field. I checked my watch. Quarter after nine. After twenty minutes I caught myself dozing off. How perfect it would be to come all this way for a nap in the countryside.

Moving slowly backwards I stood up behind the big tree and stretched my legs. The change gave me a view of the fields and a sudden flash of color in the distance. I grabbed the binoculars.

Riders on horses.

Adrenaline surged through me. I crouched back down against the trunk. Could they see me? I turned the dial on the lenses; it was Ludo, Pascal and Alix. They got an earlier start then she thought.

The two men had shotguns on their backs. Pheasant hunting I guessed. Unless Alix had betrayed me? But if that were true they would have rifles instead of shotguns.

They rode toward the stone wall further up the slope and the horses bounded over it handily. They were facing away from me now. I peered around the other side of the tree and used the binoculars to look over the estate. Nothing.

I left the cover of the woods and ran across the scrub. With one hand on the gun in my pocket I gave the front door a couple of solid raps with the brass knocker. There was no response. I knocked again, glancing up toward the woods and fields beyond. I took a deep breath and tried the door handle. Locked.

I walked around the house and at the far end, closest to the barn, a basement level window had been broken and then replaced with a white painted board.

Sitting down and using both legs I gave the board a solid kick. The nails popped out of the sill and the board crashed down on the floor. With the light now streaking into the basement I turned myself over and wiggled into the frame and then dropped down. I found the board and replaced it, giving just a little push to hold it until I needed to get out again. As I did the light went out. I felt like I was breaking into a dungeon. A flashlight would have been handy.

I took out my lighter and walked with it in my outstretched arm. In the distance, the length of the estate, was a bright spot where I guessed the other window was. After what felt like an eternity I came to a staircase. At the top some dim light shown from under a door.

I prayed it wouldn't be locked.

I thumbed the latch and the door creaked open. On the other side I found myself in the working part of a kitchen.

A huge stone sink, table, and a collection of pots and pans hung from iron hooks in the low ceiling. A solid oak chopping block looked like it had been used to cut veal steaks since the fifteenth century.

I made my way out to the dining room and then through the billiard room and library. Only a few books rested in the dark oak bookcases built into the walls. The rare works that once lined these bookshelves had probably been sold off by the generations preceding Ludo's purchase.

The one locked door had an old skeleton keyhole. My lock picks wouldn't work here. I made my way to the front hall and found a closet. I unraveled one of the metal hangers and made a hard little bend at the tip using a crack in the locked door and then pushed it into the keyhole until I felt resistance. I turned it and slowly pulled back the wire until it caught on something and twisted with a final click.

As I opened the door there was a rattle of pans in the kitchen. The sound stopped me. The cook no doubt. This could make my departure more challenging. I closed the door and went over to the broad desk. Ludo was a fastidious man. His office was tidy and his desk was cleared of everything but a photostat and a framed photo of Alix with her cheeks rouged. Was he really in love with her?

I looked at the photocopy. An official memo from the chief of the Police judiciaire. *Sujet d'enquête de corruption.* I did not recognize the name on the form.

Somebody had tipped off Ludo about an investigation and my guess was that he just recently shared the news with Pascal.

I tried the desk drawers but they were all empty. How strange. Who had empty desk drawers? I looked around for a safe, but there was nothing, no picture on the wall, no closet. Maybe it was in his bedroom? Did I have time to check upstairs? What if I opened a door and found Ludo's driver?

I closed the office door behind me and took the curved stairwell as quietly as I could. In both directions were doorways. On a hunch I went to the furthest on the left. The one that would command a view of the driveway and road in the distance. One of Ludo's brash suits was laid out on the bed. But this bedroom was nothing like the one at his "safe house." No gold satin sheets. Just a smallish bed, a dresser, a nightstand with a bottle of pills.

I looked in the closet but only found a shotgun that looked like it might have come with the house, and some of Alix's dresses and shoes. The thought of sharing a woman with Ludo was nauseating. I checked under the painting on the wall and everywhere else I could think a safe might be. Nothing.

Something caught my eye out the window and I looked to see a shaggy wolfhound being walked by a man in a black suit. So that's where the chauffer had been. At least I could check all the rooms now.

I made my way back to the staircase and tried the other hallway. One room had an open suitcase on the bed. This must be Pascal's. Like the rest, there was no safe.

A place like this would have a massive attic. I checked the bedrooms for an extra door and found it in the last room facing the back fields. I went to the window first and looked out toward the woods. There was nothing on the horizon, but that didn't mean the riders weren't on their way back or in the barn.

I took the stairwell to a room full of dusty boxes, old furniture, even an upright piano. How the hell did that get up here? I pulled open a few boxes, drawers and even the top of the piano. Nothing. Nothing had been touched in a generation.

A woman's voice called up from the stairwell and my heart skipped a beat. I froze like a statue and tried not to breath.

"Y'a quelqu'un?"

I reached for my gun but held the piano instead to keep my balance. I wasn't about to shoot the maid. After another moment the door closed and I heard her leave the bedroom. I let out my breath. Would she report the attic door being open? I shouldn't wait to find out.

I very quietly took the stairs back down and after listening at the door crossed the hall. I heard voices and looked out the window. Ludo, Pascal and Alix were walking their horses to the barn. Ludo's driver watched with the dog. I didn't like my odds. The safe bet was to get out of the house, but I hated leaving empty handed. There had to be another way. Maybe Pascal knew where the Gestapo file was.

I went down the hall, opened the door to his room and took a seat in the chair by the window. It was fifteen minutes before I heard footsteps in the hall. I listened as the floor boards creaked in the opposite direction. Ludo?

Not long after I heard someone else on the landing. Then the door before me opened and Pascal entered. He closed the door behind him, oblivious, and took off his hat.

"Have a nice ride?" I asked, lifting my gun.

"Who the hell are you?" he bawled.

I put a finger to my lips. "Or I'll permanently shut your mouth. Sit on the bed."

Pascal hesitated like a man not used to taking orders but did as I instructed.

"Answer my questions and you'll leave this place alive. Give me any bullshit, and believe me I'll enjoy putting a bullet in you."

He nodded and swallowed hard.

"You're a kingmaker in the PNU, correct?"

He gave a tight shrug. "I'm a faithful party member."

"I heard you pull the strings."

Pascal shrugged again. "People listen to my advice."

"Answer me this then," I said. "Ludo is blackmailing one of your party's rising stars, counselor Marc Bechard. So why are you two so chummy?"

He started with an "I don't know what you're talking about," but rethought his cooperation when I put the magnum against his right kneecap.

"Look," he said. "Marc's a politician. An ambitious one, but just one of many. The party could have cut him loose and moved on. If Ludo wanted political favors, then we needed some dirty work in return. The kind of stuff that couldn't be traced back to us."

"Like killing Osval Delage and Liana Cole two years ago?" I said, prodding his knee with the gun.

Pascal waved the accusation away. "I had nothing to do with that. Ludo didn't tell me a thing about it," he said hotly. "He just asked if I had a man to spare. He needed a fall guy he said. Osval was a degenerate, a queer. I told him Ludo needed him for a job. I had no idea he meant to kill Osval so the girl's death would get pinned on the communists." Reading the skepticism on my face, he continued hurriedly. "That was to cover his own ass. I could care less if Ludo lost his file on Marc."

"Did you know Marc used to go by the name Gustave Dubroc? That he was a finger man for the Gestapo?"

"I didn't before I saw Ludo's file."

"Do you know where it is? The file?"

Pascal shook his head. "Honestly, I wish I did."

"Have you seen Ludo use a safe here?" I asked.

"No, I don't think he has one. I've never seen one," he said nervously. "I think the file is at his café. He said something about it being in a vault."

I wished I didn't believe him.

"Look," I said. "I'm going to need you to stay in your room a while."

Pascal nodded enthusiastically.

I stood up and put my magnum in my waistband. "See that closet there," I said, pointing to the corner.

Pascal turned his head to follow. When he turned back

my fist was already speeding toward his face. It collided with his jaw. Pascal flopped back onto the bed — out cold.

"Stay," I said, rubbing my knuckles.

I checked his pockets, patted him down and took a look in his suitcase. He had no weapon. Nothing under the pillow or mattress either. I pocketed his car keys just in case. All I had to do now was sneak out.

I stepped into the hallway and started to the stairwell just as Alix left her room and headed in my direction. She stopped short when she saw me. Then she nodded toward her room.

"Where's Ludo?" I asked, closing the door behind us.

"Downstairs."

"And the driver?"

"Having a drink with Ludo," she said. "What are you going to do?"

"Get the hell out of here," I answered. "With your help."

She looked relieved and then came closer and kissed my cheek. She held her lips there like Liana used to do and then turned away.

"What is it?"

She tried stifling back tears and started convulsing. She took deep breaths but couldn't stop.

I pulled her to me and shushed her like a baby until her breathing calmed. She wiped her face with her sleeve. I wanted to kiss her. To tell her we'd find a way through this together. But I knew there was something we couldn't overcome. I sat on the bed and dropped my hands from her sides.

"Did you know?" I asked.

"Know what?" she said, regaining herself.

I lifted my head to look in her eyes. "That he killed your sister."

My face burned from the icy sting of her slap. "How dare you," she hissed.

"Then tell me I'm wrong," I said. "Tell me you weren't Ludo's lover knowing what he'd done."

"I didn't know," she said, looking down at me. Her whole body went limp and she sunk to her knees in front of me. "I didn't know," she repeated.

She lay her head on my lap and I caressed her hair as she cried.

"Ludo gave me a chance," she said in a whisper. "I was a collaborator, I had nothing. And *I didn't know* what he'd done, I swear. He said he felt sorry for me, losing my sister, that's why he gave me a job. When he'd ask if you and Papa had found Liana's killer, I thought it was concern. But over time, seeing all the cruelty he inflicted, I knew he was incapable of pity. When you came to the casino and said his man tried to kill you, I felt something turn over inside me. I knew it was true. But I tried not to believe it. I couldn't change what happened. I didn't want to lose all I'd worked for. I didn't want to lose you or Papa. I swear it, Eli. I swear it. I should have told you I was having doubts, but…"

"It's okay," I said.

I knew Alix wanted my forgiveness, but she'd have to find that herself. I lifted her up and helped her to sit on the bed.

"I believe you," I said.

She nodded and dried her eyes some more. "Don't hate me."

"I never could," I said, holding her to me.

"Now tell me what you want me to do. Anything," she said. "And I'll find his safe, I promise. Come find me at the casino in a couple days."

"I will."

She put her hand on my face a moment and smiled wistfully.

"When you're ready," I told her. "Go downstairs and draw them away from the kitchen. The dog too. I'll get out the way I came in."

She took a moment to collect herself and then stood up and smoothed her dress. She bent over and kissed me and then nodded that she was ready. I nodded back and she stepped out into the hall. I heard her steps until she reached the stairs, then they stopped. There was a commotion and a muffled scream.

I crouched down and peeked out the door. Near the stairs something was hanging out of one of the bedrooms.

"Have you ever used a Tommy Gun?" Ludo asked as I fell back into the room. I heard a commotion on the stairs. I guessed the chauffer was taking Alix away. Her heels clattered down the stone steps.

I went over to the hearth and dragged the heavy iron fireback to the doorway.

"Never have," I replied, laying down behind it. "It's a woman's gun, isn't it?"

There was no reply.

I looked over at the window closest to me and wondered if I'd break a leg dropping out of it.

"It's good for killing women, if that's what you mean," the voice answered.

If he wanted me to lose my cool, it was working. But I didn't take the bait.

"A man who shoots an unarmed woman," I said instead. "You're a real tough guy."

"And to think you might have saved her," he sighed. "If you'd known she was a whore."

I heard him laugh from down the hall. Blood burned my face and my fists tightened.

He sprayed some bullets in my direction just in case I rushed. When it was over I crawled over to the closet and took the shotgun from the corner. I cracked it open and found two shells. If they weren't a hundred years old they should still fire. Nothing instilled fear like a shotgun blast in your direction and this one was a cannon.

Getting Ludo to spend some cartridges would be helpful. I stretched myself out from behind the fireback and hooked my arm around the door jam and fired my magnum.

"Hey, asshole!" I yelled.

His reply was instant and I held my head as wood shards burst from the wall. I fired blindly with my Colt and then cocked the shotgun barrels as another barrage of bullets crashed through the hallway.

How many fucking bullets did a Tommy Gun hold? I listened for the sound of him changing his magazine. Nothing but the ringing in my ears. I stood up and tucked my magnum in my waistband. "God, let these shells work," I prayed before jumping out the door and firing a blast down the hall.

I charged forward, saw which room Ludo had pulled back into, and blasted a hole through the wall where I hoped he was standing.

191

I heard him curse as I ducked into the closest room. The Tommy Gun came back around the corner and sprayed hell rain along the floorboards and walls. There was noise on the stairwell and I followed right behind. Ludo went straight across the entrance hall downstairs. I fired a shot at his running figure, hoping it would keep him from turning around too soon. From the top of the staircase something caught my eye out the large entranceway window. Coming down the dirt road near the barn was a red truck. What were the odds it was bringing Ludo's local goon squad?

I went for broke down the stairs and pulled open the massive front door. A bullet zinged right through it, inches from my head. The truck was barreling toward the estate and I could see men standing in the back.

I dug out Pascal's keys and went right for the Talbot Lago.

I worried a quick second about Alix but then started the car and stuck it in gear like I was at the starting line of the Grand Prix. In the rearview I saw Ludo and his driver looking after me, but if they fired I didn't hear it. By the time I got into town my adrenaline was sapped.

I stopped at the hotel to retrieve my bottle of Armagnac and then made the long drive to Henri's.

Zelie waved from the garden as I parked the very conspicuous car behind the barn. I met her in the yard.

"Country life suits you," I said, giving her a hug.

"Madame Chastain," she said, gushing, as if that explained everything. "Farming is dirty, but not in the way I'm used to." She gave me an exaggerated wink.

I shook my head. "You could be in vaudeville."

192

"Nobody came to the farm," she said. "But I kept the shotgun in my room."

"Not loaded I hope."

"I keep the bullets in my pocket." She pulled two shot-gun shells from her denim overalls.

"Good girl."

"Want to help pull weeds?"

"Sure," I said, letting her drag me into the garden.

A couple hours later JP drove up in his van and we all went inside.

"Cosette made Daube de Boeuf. Do you want to wait for Remy?" Henri asked.

"We'll eat," said JP, sitting down at the table.

A few minutes later Cosette came in and set the tureen of stew on the table. Zelie followed with a basket of sliced bread. After we finished eating, the two spaniels announced the arrival of Remy.

He came in, set his bag in the corner and dished himself some dinner.

"*Marc* kept regular hours at his office on rue de Rivoli," JP repeated for Remy. "I checked with his secretary about meeting him in a few days. She said he would not be available. I told her it was about Gustave Dubroc and that I'd be in touch."

"That should do it," Remy agreed.

"It better," JP said with a short laugh.

"My forger friend said the file will be done the day after tomorrow."

I relayed what Pascal said about the party working with Ludo in exchange for dirty work, and how the Gestapo file on Gustave was probably in a vault somewhere at the café.

I also told them Alix was still with Ludo. I left out the bit about the Tommy Gun.

JP looked as worried as I expected.

"I don't think Ludo will hurt her," I said. "Alix certainly didn't think so."

"I doubt Ludo is any match for her anyways," JP answered.

Chapter Sixteen

IN THE MORNING ZELIE CAME DOWNSTAIRS in her work clothes and after buttering a piece of bread went out to the garden. I sat on the porch and watched her and Cosette picking green beans. Zelie gave me a disparaging look and waved me over. If I was going to be a gentleman farmer someday I should know how to get my hands dirty. Cosette directed me to the tomatoes.

"We need *red* ones for dinner," she instructed with a wink.

"Not green?"

She handed me a basket. The tall tomato plants were tied to wooden stakes. Kneeling in the soft earth and smelling the summer morning reminded me of helping Liana turn the soil. She loved growing things in this garden. I felt that sinking feeling. How could it be that I'd never kneel beside her again?

When I was back in the States I could plant a garden for her. If it was mine, it would also be Liana's. Wasn't part of my soul our lives together? Wasn't the love we shared part of me? I remembered the way we looked at each other, the way we kissed.

How could I have ever doubted the truth of that love?

Because she eventually lied to me, betrayed me, left me.

What was that against the enormity of all we'd shared?

There *never* were any answers. Not from me, not from Liana — even if she were alive. Everything I didn't know about her, all the unanswered questions — didn't change us. It didn't change the love we'd found.

Zelie put her hand on mine and "helped" pull the fat tomato I had been holding from the vine.

"You okay?"

"Fine," I answered, offering a smile.

"Cosette is making ratatouille."

"Maybe you should watch and learn," I teased.

"You'd like that, wouldn't you? I'm not going to be your maid in America."

I laughed. "The idea never crossed my mind. But I think the young man you someday marry might expect you to know how to cook."

"Well, somebody's going to be very disappointed," she smiled. She reached for another tomato and whispered, "Why do I feel nothing will go as planned?"

"Because nothing ever does," I said without thinking.

She kneeled with me in the dirt. "But I so want it to."

"So do I, Zelie."

She hugged me with all her strength and then got up quickly and went back to Cosette.

Two days passed in tranquil, quiet routine. I had coffee on the porch and remembered doing the same with Liana. Passing her a cigarette, both of us enchanted by life on the farm. And later, in the evenings, we'd drink and dance with Henri and Cosette to blues records or Liana would play her ukulele, smiling as she sang in her smokey voice.

JP, who all these years had acted like I'd stolen away his favorite daughter, now stood outside in the evenings and talked about his regrets, the mistakes he made with his marriage and daughters. The disappointment he felt in himself for fixing the cars, heaters and toilets of the Nazi occupier. He did it to keep his daughters fed, but it ate away at his soul. I doubted he'd told anyone else how much.

"Liana resented being dependent on Nazis," he said. "I tried to rationalize. But I don't think she ever understood."

He lit another cigarette.

"You did what you had to," I said.

"That's what I told myself."

We watched the pigs root in the mud.

"Her affair," he said, giving me a quick look. "It only lives in you now. There's no pain or regret in the Kingdom."

He put his cigarette out against the wood fence. "She's gone. We can only remember her. Why hold the hurt above everything else that was beautiful?"

The following evening JP confirmed an appointment for 10:00 am at Gustave's office. The house was quiet, like the silence before a storm.

We decided to spend the night in the city.

Zelie never came down, but I knew she would be watching us from her window. Henri poured us two espressos to keep us awake.

"Good luck," he said.

We drank them quickly and shook hands.

"Give our thanks to Cosette," JP said. He pulled his nephew into a hug and patted him hard on the back.

"I will."

JP led us out.

"I have thought on our plan," he said. We pulled out onto the road but JP didn't elaborate. The orange sun was setting on a clear blue horizon. But the air felt heavy and I felt choked and anxious. This was like D-Day all over again.

JP lit a cigarette. "If anything goes wrong, I want you to just keep to the plan. Don't worry about me. Get the file, kill Ludo. These are the only important things."

What JP was asking of me was easier said than done. I didn't want Alix to be right about all this.

"We'll get the file."

He seemed less than satisfied with my answer. But he didn't say anything else. Instead, he chain-smoked all the way to Paris, and when his pack ran out we stopped in Drancy to get more.

We spent the last leg of the trip figuring out what to do if Ludo called our bluff. We settled with dynamite. For the sake of anyone in the café or his apartment building I hoped he showed.

We were to meet Remy at 8:00 p.m. to get the fake documents. I was confident in our plan but my stomach was queasy. JP dug a bag of ginger candies from the glovebox.

"We will have a drink at the Ritz bar tonight," he said grandly.

"The Ritz?"

"Bourgeois I know, but I've always wanted to go."

"So have I. Liana and I talked about it, but somehow never did."

"Then she would approve."

JP parked the van on Place Vendôme. The maitre d' gave

us a look he probably reserved for American tourists in short sleeves but let us through.

The bar was bigger than I expected and modern. The chairs, tables, everything in the latest style. Behind the marble-top bar was a long mural by Picasso.

We took two stools and let the place wash over us. The people here were not JP's people, and they weren't mine. But maybe for an evening we could all share in the decadence. When the barman came over, JP ordered a beer but then quickly waved it off.

"A Negroni," he said. "Something else I've never tried."

"Liana's favorite," I told him before ordering a vodka martini.

"Somehow I knew that," he smiled.

The barman brought the drinks and JP elevated his.

"The years before the war, when my girls were young, were the happiest in my life. And I know for Liana, it was the years after. The ones with you, Eli."

We tapped glasses. It was the nicest thing he'd ever said.

There was plenty to talk about but we did little. It was enough to be in a fine bar on the eve of who knew what. I wished we'd done it years ago.

At eight Remy pulled up in a blue Citroen.

"I've borrowed a car, and a gun," he said. He pulled a folder from his satchel.

He handed it to me and I flipped it open. It looked just the way I imagined a Gestapo file would. Except the insides were charred to a crisp, only the tops of carbon papers and the edges of some photographs survived. But the name Gustave Dubroc was visible on the cover and on the front sheet.

"It would fool me," I said.

JP took it from my hands and looked it over. He slapped Remy on the shoulder. "This is excellent work."

Remy nodded. "We ambush them at Gustave's office. I looked the building over today, the stairwell is perfect. JP shows the councilor this file and instructs him to call Ludo right away. If their conversation goes the way it should, Ludo will deny the file is destroyed and offer to show Gustave the real one."

"Then we wait," I said.

"Once Gustave makes his call," Remy said, "JP can find us at the café next door."

JP nodded. "Okay."

"Friends of mine are staking out Ludo's office and apartment. When Ludo's on his way they'll call the payphone."

We watched Remy walk back to his car.

"It will be hard to sleep tonight. We could go to another bar," JP suggested.

I was going to say we needed to be sharp, but the prospect of staring at the ceiling for the next ten hours changed my mind. We walked across the street to a place that was mostly empty. We took a table with a good view of the entrance. The few men sitting or standing at the counter paid us no attention.

JP went to the bar and brought back two beers.

"Probably horse piss," he said with a snort.

He was right, but it would do.

"I keep wondering if we're missing something about tomorrow," I said.

"Maybe we are," JP said, frowning at the taste of the beer. "But there's nothing to do about it now."

I supposed he was right.

"Where are Myriam and Emilienne now?" I asked to change the subject. "Will you see them soon?"

"Yes, they arrive in a few days. I wish she had been closer to her sisters. They were pretty well grown up when she was born. Maybe it's for the best," he said. Then shaking his head. "What will this world offer her? I pray not another war. Or a life of servitude like my eldest. I wish I could have done more for her. For all of them."

I searched for something to say, but nothing could change JP's perception of himself as a father. How many others had been defeated by the war? How many daughters died or were broken by hardship? How many fathers returned from some prison or labor camp to find their sons and daughters gone from them forever?

"You did your best. They know that," I finally said.

He just grunted and took a drink.

JP's idea of bedding was work blankets he'd borrowed from the Union. I managed to fall asleep sometime in the early morning. JP woke me at half past eight. He looked like he had no sleep at all. There was an espresso cup and several cigarette butts on the kitchen floor.

"I already went out," he said. "But you were sleeping."

I nodded and pushed myself up. My shoulders and hips were sore. I found the bathroom and changed my under-clothes.

JP was standing by the door with another cigarette. He had the doctored Gestapo folder under his arm. "We can sit at the café until ten."

We took the metro over to the Fourth. The morning rush was unexpected. The rest of the world had disappeared in my mind. I'd forgotten other people would be going about their business.

The café was busy, which gave us some cover. JP looked nervously at the pensioner talking on the phone in the door-way. He shrugged his shoulders at me.

"It'll be alright," I said. My watch read 9:30.

Remy arrived and stood by the door.

JP stabbed out his tenth cigarette of the morning and got up from the table. "I'm going to take a leak."

The lady hung up the phone and about three seconds later it rang. She turned back from the exit to answer it, but Remy managed to get around her and pick up.

I stood next to him to listen.

"Ludo arrived at the café," the voice said.

"Good," Remy replied.

"There's something else. A woman is with him."

It had to be Alix.

"Should we continue as planned?" the man asked.

JP was returning from the bathroom. He saw me and I motioned for him to come over.

"Alix arrived with Ludo at the café," I told him.

He took a second to absorb the news. "So we deal with Ludo and Alix walks free."

It sounded a little optimistic, but not impossible.

"Yes, it's still on," Remy conveyed.

The phone clicked.

JP looked at his watch and nodded toward the window. "Right on time."

Gustave was getting out of a black sedan just a few meters up the street. He had a creased but handsome face, with hair that was grey on the sides. His suit was expensive and I guessed he was as smug an asshole as he looked.

This time when JP lit a cigarette, I had one with him. After he stubbed it out, he took a deep breath.

"I'll be right here," I said.

Then he was out the door. After twenty seconds I followed and leaned against the wall next to the café. I could see JP get to the entrance of the building next door and go in. Assuming the councilor saw him right away, we should expect his return in fifteen or twenty minutes. Every minute after that I'd be nervous.

I smoked another Gauloises despite the dryness in my throat. The street was busy with cars and pedestrians. Nobody seemed to be hanging around except me. I scanned the buildings across the street and then noticed someone sitting in a parked car. I saw him more clearly when the traffic broke. He was looking at the building JP had gone into.

Was he waiting for an appointment or was he here for another reason? I went back into the café and sat with Remy at a table by the window. I could see the man in the car light a cigarette and roll the window down an inch. He exhaled the smoke in a bored way. There was something routine about his manner. As if waiting in cars was his job.

I didn't like it.

I checked my watch. Ten minutes. The councilor might have had a scheduled appointment. Maybe JP was sitting in reception.

But that seemed unlikely. JP was a liability he couldn't ignore. It occurred to me now that he may have told Ludo about it right away, especially if he thought he was about to be blackmailed again. But wouldn't he first want to know what JP wanted?

I was pulling at strings. It took all my restraint not to pace the floor.

Another five minutes dribbled by before the phone rang. Remy bolted up and answered it while I listened.

"The car is on its way. But Ludo's not in it, just the woman."

"Was she carrying anything?" Remy asked.

"Yes, a briefcase."

"How many bodyguards?"

"Two including the driver," the man answered.

"Okay, well done."

I looked back across the street. The man was still sitting in the car.

I wondered if Ludo had sent Alix in case of a trap. He knew we wouldn't risk the life of JP's other daughter by trying anything.

Come on JP, get down here.

I went back outside and watched the entrance of the office building like an expectant father. A woman came out the door and turned in the other direction.

Remy joined me.

"Something's wrong," I said. "JP should be back by now."

"Check it out," he said. "Third floor, first door on the right. There's a waiting room with a secretary."

I took the stairs at the end of the lobby and caught my breath before listening at the door. I cracked it open and peeked in. Nobody. The desk was empty. I took out my gun and went inside.

I put a hand on Gustave's office door and got a sense of its thickness. It was a solid last line of defense against some maniac, *like myself*. If it was locked my only recourse would be to try and shoot out the lock.

Voices. The door muffled the words but somebody was in there.

I tried turning the knob but it was locked.

Fuck.

Alix would be here soon. I considered waiting for the door to open, but I had no idea if any of Ludo's gunmen might be inside.

I made my way back to the stairs, then down to the street again without anyone coming my way. Remy hustled toward me on the sidewalk, pointing toward the intersection. A black sedan was approaching from the north.

"I think JP is trapped in the office," I said.

"What should we do?"

"We get the file," I said.

Remy nodded. Knowing the objective focused both of us.

"The stairwell," he said.

We hustled to the entrance. The sedan was crossing the intersection and continuing straight.

"They'll pull up on that side," Remy said.

We went to the second floor landing and waited. I noticed my gun hand shaking a little. I holstered it and put my hands against the wall. Deep breaths.

"Lying in wait is the worst for the nerves," Remy said. "We did it many times during the war. I'm not ashamed to tell you, many of the men pissed themselves before firing."

"I'll be alright," I said. I took a couple more breaths and felt my heart rate slow.

Remy grabbed my shoulder. A door had opened upstairs. Two men spoke at once. Orders to "shut up and walk."

Remy pulled me down the stairs. We reached the turn to the first floor landing when the front door opened. We were heading directly at Alix and two of Ludo's men.

It was Alix or JP. We couldn't get both of them.

"The file," Remy said.

I followed his lead down the rest of the steps with my gun behind my back. Ludo's men would be looking out for trouble but hadn't yet realized they'd found it.

The gap was closing. Alix fixed her wide eyes on me. We were ten yards away when she dropped the suitcase. It hit the marble floor with an echoing thunk. She followed it by quickly dropping into a crouch before kissing the floor.

The sudden move inspired the goons to reach for their guns.

I raised my Colt.

"Leave 'em," I commanded, surprised by my own voice.

They didn't. A split second to dive one way or the other might have prolonged the fight. Instead, we shot them twice before they chambered a round. Both men collapsed backwards as the report of our guns filled the room. Alix looked up from where she lay. Her eyes went wide again as she pointed behind us.

Remy pushed me left and dove right. I twisted around and saw men clacking down the stairs. I landed against the cold floor and got a bead on the bodies reaching the lobby. JP was hurled forward by one of the men, blocking my shot. A bullet cracked the tile two feet from my head. Luckily it didn't ricochet through my skull.

JP rushed toward us. I could see two men retreating behind the stairwell for cover.

There was a thick column a few yards behind me. I

squeezed off a shot and bounded toward it. Some lead cracked the column as I stood up behind it.

The only cover Remy had was staying tight against the wall. JP had pulled Alix up and was heading toward the front door. He had the suitcase.

I covered him with another shot at the stairs.

"Let's go," I yelled to Remy.

He started sliding backwards along the wall.

As I turned a blast went off like a cannon in my ear. You don't hear the shot that kills you, but my body reacted as if I'd just taken a bullet. When I lifted my head I saw JP collapse to the floor.

The shot had come from the doorway. The man from the car. He grabbed the suitcase and ran out the door. I had no shot with Alix standing in the way.

"I'll cover you," Remy said.

He fired toward the staircase as I ran to JP. Alix was on her knees beside him, holding his hand. The front of his shirt was red with blood. JP pulled her close and said something before he coughed and his arm fell. Alix beat JP's chest once with her fist and cried out.

"Alix!"

I tried to pull her up from the floor. "We have to go."

Two more shots came from the end of the lobby. Remy was running toward us.

I trained my gun on the stairwell as he got close but Ludo's men were playing it safe. Remy crouched down, checked JP's pulse, and after a moment closed his eyelids.

I took Alix by the waist with both hands but she fought me off.

"I'm staying with Papa!"

We left her crying over JP's body.

Henri understood the worst had happened when he saw us. I led them into the dining room. Cosette put her hand on top of Henri's on the table.

"I'm sorry," I said.

"He was a singular man," Henri replied, shaking his head.

Cosette, who I imagined just tolerated JP's antics over the years, started to cry. Henri wrapped his arm around her shoulders. I knew I'd have to wait to cry for JP. Sometime, when this was all over, I'd remember what a decent man he'd been.

Remy came to the doorway and waited for me to join him.

"We are a good man down," I said.

Remy nodded. "Gustave must have spoken to Ludo, he must have guessed JP was going to blackmail him."

"It's my fault," I said. "I should have seen this coming."

"I don't know," Remy said, and then nothing else.

I wasn't sure if he meant "what to do next" or "if we could win this fight." I didn't want to know. If I had to finish this myself I would.

Remy put his hand on my shoulder. "Let's talk later."

I watched as he went out the door. When it swung open again, Zelie came in. She gave me a hug.

"I'm sorry about JP."

"Thanks, Zelie."

She tilted her head against my shoulder and left it there. "Can I ask you something?"

"Sure," I answered.

"Is it over?"

I knew the answer but didn't know how to say it. Or if I should.

"It can be," I answered. "For you."

She shook her head. "I'm with you. No matter what."

"I know you are," I said, giving her a kiss on the forehead.

In the morning Henri met me in the kitchen holding the paper. Cosette came in after him.

"It's all on the front page," Henri said, slapping it down on the table. "It claims Jean-Paul was trying to assassinate Gustave, or Marc Bechard as they call him here. And that the councilor's bodyguards killed him. It says JP's accomplices are still at large. I don't think it will be long." Meaning the police would be looking for us.

"You can still get out," Cosette said. There was pleading in her soft voice. "Take the girl. Go home. Maybe someday, if you must, come back and finish this."

She put her head in her hands. Cosette never talked about what she'd suffered during the war, and I'd never asked.

Henri took me aside. "You are welcome here for as long as you need, but…"

"Tomorrow," I said. "We will end this, I promise."

I didn't want to bring them any more grief, as much as I appreciated the help.

"We will all go," I said.

I went out the front door. Remy was standing at the pasture fence looking at the cows. He turned when the door opened and I walked to him.

"I know what we must do," he said.

I was relieved. Remy had not surrendered.

"But we must work fast."

"Tell me," I said.

"Innocent people died every day during the war. And this is the same war. Ludo and Gustave committed crimes against the French people. The price is death. At all costs."

After this speech Remy needed a cigarette to calm his nerves. He handed me the pack and we smoked a minute in silence.

"Ludo's a smart man. We tried to lure him and the file to Gustave's. Now he'll expect us to either lay low or try something desperate. Instead, we run the same gambit. Today."

"How?"

"By sticking to Gustave like glue."

"You think he'll still want Ludo to prove he has his file?"

Remy nodded. "JP showed him a folder that looked just like the one he'd seen a couple years ago. Except it was burnt to a crisp. He's kicking himself right now for not meeting JP without informing Ludo first. He might have finally been out from under him."

"Then we better go."

"Now," Remy said.

I found Henri in the kitchen doing the dishes. He dried his hands when he saw me come through the door.

"We're leaving," I began. "But I want Zelie to stay, for now. If we end up dead or in prison I want you to watch out for her. She'll have no one."

Henri tossed the towel on the counter. "I know as an American you can't understand this. But if you were here when the army collapsed, when Weygand gave up on France.

I was called up to defend Seden in May of '40. One of the most modern armies in the world was being bombed to pieces by German planes. I knew the war was over then. I remember the feeling of my heart breaking. They had beaten us. We would have to live with the humiliation. But France survived. I survived. And now I have this farm, and Cosette and my life. I thank God for it every day," he said. He hit the edge of the sink with his palm.

I didn't say anything and after a moment Henri calmed down.

"Zelie can stay here, of course. We'll set her on the best course we can. But it won't be in America. It won't be with you."

I put my hand on Henri's shoulder. "Thank you. For everything."

He smiled and shook his head. "Stay alive."

"I'm going to try," I said.

He pat my arm. I thought to go find Zelie, but she didn't need another goodbye. I didn't either.

On the way to Paris I thought about what Henri had said. *Not winning this war.* That's what he had meant. He had lived with it. Why couldn't I?

But my path had led me through the war, to Liana. And now to vengeance. I had no interest in finding another way.

Our first stop in Paris was on the outskirts. I took over driving in the city, down Cours de Vincennes to Gare de Lyon.

"We need a new car," I said.

Remy got out and said to meet him at the corner. I locked the door, put the key behind the back tire and walked to rue de Bercy. Five minutes later Remy pulled up in a Peugeot 203 and let me in.

"Nice," I said.

"Only the best," he smiled.

We parked at the corner that faced Gustave's office building.

After three long hours of waiting for something to happen I got out to stretch my legs. At the intersection ahead a black sedan pulled up to the corner. Yannick was behind the wheel. I turned on a dime and got back in the car. The sedan passed us and crossed the intersection.

"Yannick," I said, pointing.

Remy leaned forward and squinted into the windshield. "You're sure?"

"It was him."

"Alone?"

"Yes."

We both watched for any movement but he just sat idling alongside the office building.

"Taking Gustave to Ludo's?"

"Maybe. But what would be even better than actually meeting?"

"Having Yannick show Gustave he still has his file."

"It's possible."

"We need to find out," Remy said.

"There," I said, pointing out Gustave leaving his building.

Remy started the car.

I watched as the councilor got into the back seat of the sedan. It pulled away fast and Remy stalled getting out from the curb. A white Renault got ahead of us and crawled through the intersection.

Remy followed on his bumper and when we were in the middle of the next block he put the Peugeot into second gear and jolted us into the oncoming lane.

The man gave us the *bras d'honneur* as we cut him off.

After taking a left, we saw the sedan continue straight through the next intersection. It went another two blocks.

"This isn't the way to Ludo's," I said.

At a square with a military statue in the middle the sedan took another left and pulled over.

"He'll show Gustave the file now, where he can keep a gun on him."

"Do we take them?" Remy asked.

"We'll get Yannick after he drops Gustave off. We just need the file."

Remy nodded but his grimace showed disappointment. He pulled the car up before the corner.

Then the back door of the sedan opened and Gustave exited.

"I guess Yannick told him to find his own way back."

The sedan pulled away and Remy took the corner fast. We passed Gustave who was walking toward us. His head was hung low.

"Being a scumbag is taking its toll," Remy said, speeding up.

"We need to do this before he reaches Ludo's café," I reminded him.

"Want me to knock him off the road?"

"Can you do it without killing anyone?"

"We have about ten blocks to decide."

"Then do it," I said.

There was some traffic. When Remy saw the sedan go straight, he took a left, sped down the street and made the next two rights so hard I thought the car might roll over. He pulled up to the next intersection and I jumped out to look around the corner.

"He's two cars back," I said, getting back in.

When the sedan was next at the stop sign Yannick looked both ways and pulled into the intersection.

Remy jammed the car into gear and propelled us like a catapult directly into Yannick's side door. The impact jolted me forward and I caught my head in my arms as I hit the dash.

Remy bounced off the steering wheel like a rag doll. We were stunned but got ourselves out of the car. The sedan was crushed. I pulled out my gun and approached the passenger side door. I felt like I was moving in slow motion and had gone deaf.

I pulled open the door. Yannick was on his side, a bloody gash across his forehead. His lower half was pinned. He saw me and reached under his jacket. I pulled the trigger. His head was knocked backwards and then came forward to rest against the wheel.

On the floor was a suitcase. I took it. Remy had successfully disengaged our car from the wreck and backed up the street. The engine whined and gasped, but ran. I noticed people gathering around the black sedan. Some looked at us as we retreated, their mouths open in disbelief.

Remy didn't stop at the next intersection and in a minute the accident was out of sight. He looked at me and then down at the suitcase.

I turned it around on my lap and pulled up the latches. Inside there was a brown file that looked like the one JP had shown Gustave yesterday.

I opened it. This time the pages were complete, so were the photographs. A few pages deep were three photos of Gael Favret. One was of him exiting the house used by the Resistance at 36 rue St. Augustin. The duplicate to the picture Gustave had lost under his desk at the Sorbonne. The other two photos were of Gael sitting with a man on a park bench.

"Jean Lamarche," Remy said, taking a quick look. "One of the leaders of the Paris underground. Killed by the Gestapo just before the breakout of '44."

The rest of the pages were reports, some by Gustave, others by the Gestapo. A trader in the lives of his fellow countrymen. Death was too good for him. He should be drawn and quartered. This file would accomplish that in its own way.

"Take us to *Le Monde*, on rue d'Italie," I said.

Le Monde was the biggest newspaper in France.

Remy took a left. "What is our next move?" he asked.

"We get Ludo," I said. But even as the words came out I knew it wasn't entirely true. Some kind of understanding had finally come.

When Remy pulled up in front of *Le Monde* I handed him the file. "Know anybody in there?" I asked.

"Not personally," he answered. "But I've read a guy who isn't afraid of exposing French collaborators."

"Give this to him."

Remy nodded and took the file. "What will you do?"

"I'll find Ludo. Then we can make a plan."

215

Remy opened his door but didn't get out. Instead, he shook my hand. "I hope you find him," he said. And then he was out the door.

The faint whisper of what needed to be done became a drumbeat in my head. To kill the king, the knight had to be sacrificed. It was the only way, and always was. But there was one last thing I needed to do.

I drove over the Pont Neuf and parked outside my apartment. It was such an obvious place to look for me I figured the CIA and Ludo's men wouldn't waste their time.

I was surprised to find my apartment just as I left it, nobody had even bothered busting in. The other reel-to-reel tape I'd found in Liana's boxes was in the bedside stand. If I was going to spend some time with Liana's voice, I figured it should be the tape I hadn't heard yet.

I took a last look around the apartment. It was a dead place without Liana. I wouldn't miss it and nothing here would miss me. Except maybe Liana's letters in the ammo box. Would Alix or Zelie come to collect them? Would they see why there was no other way for me but to finish what my love had started?

I had a glass of water from the tap and went out to the balcony. I supposed I would miss Paris. At least all it had been in better times. I set the glass down, hitting the table like a judge's gavel. This would be the last time I'd set foot in this place.

I left the car where it was and walked up to the Sorbonne. It was a beautiful day and somehow the little time ahead of me was enough. Paris was the sun, the trees, the people, and the promise of bread, wine and love. Three thousand days of it or one afternoon. In some ways it was all the same.

There's always a reason not to do what needs to be done. For me, it was Zelie. I was a part of her life now. She'd never understand me leaving her for someone who was already dead. She'd think I couldn't live in a world without Liana. But I could. It was living in a world where Liana's killer breathed the same air. That was a place I'd never be free.

I flicked on the lights in the gallery and made my way to the back. The tree collected the light and warmed it as it refracted from branch to branch. I opened the drawer, used the rewind switch to make the tape taut against the empty uptake reel and pulled it out. I put it behind the recorder and then strung the tape from my pocket. I pressed play with the drawer open and then sat down on the floor.

"*My Dearest Eli,*" Liana's voice began.

"*It's only been two days since we kissed goodbye, but I miss you in a way I can't describe. Imagining you on some hulking ship, taking you further and further from me every hour, breaks my heart. I wish you could hear me as I say your name over the ocean and know I'm with you and that neither of us is helpless, only hopelessly in love...*"

I bolted upright and stopped the tape. My heart was racing. Liana's first letter. This tape must have been a first draft of sorts, when she read the letters as they were written. I felt electrified. Why had she disarranged the words for the final version? Because it was too personal? Or maybe for her the art was in the words and not the message?

I switched the lever again and sat back down. I had reread some of these letters in the years since being written, but not all of them. To hear Liana reading them made my eyes well up with tears. I let the pitch of her voice carry me back to our first year together and all the ways we fought against the tides pulling us apart. We thought our love had won.

For an hour I listened as the tone fluctuated between optimism and defeat to final elation. I recognized the final letter —the one Liana sent after I'd telegrammed her that I was on my way back to France. She wrote me anyways, because she had needed to put her excitement into some form, and I read it a month later when my parents returned it. When I heard, "I will see you so soon my love," I got up, rubbed my legs and reached for the off switch. As I did, I heard Liana say my name. She repeated, "Eli," and I stood back from the machine.

"I wish I'd had the courage to tell you sooner, when this letter might have made a difference. Instead, I can only hurt you, and burden you with the same terrible weight I carry for having broken my promise, for having been unfaithful to the man I love.

I wish I had told you I was suffocating. That sometimes I needed to feel neither loving, or dutiful, or faithful. But I didn't know how to step off the pedestal, how to be anything but perfect for you. I even blamed you for what I had done. It was easy. I blamed you for not seeing what I never showed you. And the shame of that is something I must carry alone. Because I cannot bear to see your eyes when they know the truth. I know that beautiful way you look at me, like I'm the light in all the darkness, will go cold.

Our one and only hope is to let you hate me. Because

218

without the truth of what I've done between us, there is nothing but a lie. That must not be our fate.

Even if you can never forgive me.

I wish more than anything this hadn't happened. If only I could make you believe how much I want to choose you, Eli. If only you could believe, even after all I've done, that I never want to be without you. That I know you are the true love of my life."

The player scrolled through empty tape as I stared at it, unable to move, until it clicked off. I heard Liana's voice say again "I never want to be without you," and wished I could hold her, tell her no matter who she was, or who she'd become, or how she wanted to live, I'd always love her. That she could have trusted me with all of her.

How could she not have known?

When I was ready for the tears to come, they somehow didn't. Only a long exhale, like breath I'd been holding for two long years.

Slowly, I became conscious again of where I was. I rewound the tape to the beginning of the last letter and clipped it out. I wound her confession around an empty reel and put it in my pocket. I knew I shouldn't change Liana's art but I wanted anyone who listened to the sound of the glass tree to know the kind of love we had. I wanted us to be remembered for it. As I pushed the drawer closed, I wondered what would happen to all the memories we had made together, after we were both gone. Liana once told me love traveled like sound waves into the cosmos and would never cease, even after we died. I hoped it was true.

*

Before the corner at rue du Louvre I parked the car and tucked the car keys under the seat. I took out my Colt and checked the clip. Most of the gun went into my front pocket, I kept my hand on it.

I crossed the street and started to feel it. Everything in focus, colors brightening. I was becoming a soldier again. I breathed deeply to stave off panic and tried to imagine Liana beside me. "Courage," she said. I saw her ahead of me on the staircase, looking back.

The sign over the café door was only a few yards away.

I took out my Colt, racked the slide, and pulled open the door.

A man smiled at me from behind the counter. An older man at a table gaped. I moved to the archway leading to the back room. A voice behind me — "Arrêtez!"

I walked through.

Two tables of six men. The left with Ludo standing at the head giving the day's orders. Then silence as he looked up at me. For a fraction of a second he saw his mistake, the one thing he hadn't planned for. Around the table men began to stand and reach for their weapons.

I raised my gun to Ludo's chest.

Then Alix stood up in front of him. I hadn't even seen her.

"Drop it," she said.

Several of the men now had their guns trained on me.

I lowered the gun to the floor. She came toward me now. The men watched, some smiling at my predicament. Ludo was shaking his head.

"You almost got me, Eli," he said. "Such sacrifice. I'm flattered my death means so much to you."

Alix leaned down in front of me and picked up the gun. When she stood, she gave me a quick glance. It told me everything. The men sat back down in their chairs as she lifted the gun to my head and moved behind me.

Ludo chuckled as he approached. "Surprised?" he gloated. He got within spitting distance. "Why let you live?"

"You shouldn't," I answered. "But my wife, that was a mistake."

"My sister," Alix said.

The sudden horror on Ludo's face lasted only a second before his head split open and his body collapsed to the floor. The sudden blast ringing in my ears froze the men at the tables. When they registered what had just happened they melted lower in their seats, their eyes on me and on Alix, until one of them reached for the croissant on his plate.

The king was dead. If they managed to stay alive one of them might be the new king.

"Go," Alix said.

I backed away to the arch and turned. The man from behind the counter was standing with a shotgun. But it was pointed down. If nobody was going to shoot me in that room, he sure as hell wasn't either.

Outside, I walked. Calmly at first, but then my pace quickened until I was running to the corner. Suddenly I wanted to live.

Living was something. Even without Liana.

Chapter Seventeen

"OUR LOCAL CONSTABLE STOPPED BY TODAY," Henri said. I'd parked the Talbot Lago near the barn and he'd come to greet me. "He wanted to offer his condolences for JP."

But we both knew what he was really looking for.

"Did he see Zelie?"

"He saw her in the garden. Summer help, I told him, from Paris."

"Somebody will come back," I said.

"Maybe, but things move slowly here. You have a few days."

In the morning Henri drove into town for a paper. Nothing about Gustave. Did nobody at *Le Monde* believe the file was real? The lower front page reported the death of one of Paris's notable gangsters. It said Ludo Orban's body had been found near the river by sanitation workers. A criminal associate, Yannick Vautrin, was also found dead in his car after what witnesses described as a hit and run collision. There was nothing about Alix. I hoped she was somewhere safe and *not* the new head of the Paris mafia.

I went out to the garden later with Zelie and Cosette but only managed to watch them work. Jean-Paul would have been pleased. I wished he was here. I wanted him to tell me it was worth the sacrifice. I laid back in the grass. The cool blades brushed my neck. The cool air gave me some hope.

Later in the day, Alix called. I brought the phone to the porch.

"Jean-Paul's last words," she said. "'Alix Chastain, La Couturière.' My calling card when I was a child. A favorite saying of his over the years. His last thought, still hoping for me to change."

"Alix...you saved my life."

"I wasn't going to lose anyone else."

"What will you do?" I asked.

"My mother and sister are here. I don't know yet. Dressmaking?"

I heard her laugh. "Why not?" I chuckled.

"I want you to do something for me, Eli. About Liana. Stop asking — you know the answer. I love you too. JP loved you like a son."

"I know."

"You'll remember me, won't you?"

"I promise."

Henri didn't need to go out for the next day's paper. It was delivered in person by my friend Bill Colman.

"Donovan figured out where you were holed up," he said with a smile and handshake.

I introduced him to Henri and Cosette, who came outside and looked at the paper he'd brought. The headline was shared between the death of Gustave Dubroc, alias Marc Bechard, by suicide and the Gestapo file detailing his betrayals during the war. A reporter at *Le Monde* apparently called him for comment on the story. An hour later he put a gun to his head.

Bill put his arm around my shoulder and led me away from the house.

"You really did it this time," he said with a laugh.

"I don't know what you're talking about," I said with a straight face.

Bill laughed so hard he went red. "Either way, I've been instructed to get you back to the States immediately."

"How immediate?"

"Tonight. You're off to England via yacht, then on to New York on the Queen Elizabeth."

When Zelie came out of the house, I waved her over.

"I have some rather heavy baggage," I said. "You remember my adopted daughter."

"How could I forget?" Bill said, shaking her hand. "I'll have to see about your lost American passport Miss Zelie."

"Zelie Cole," I said.

Bill chuckled. "Of course."

"I like that," she said, smiling.

"I grabbed a few things of yours from the office and your apartment," Bill said. "There's a couple bags in the car."

"Did you..." I started.

Bill nodded. "Got it. And enough clothes to get you home. The rest, if you want, can be shipped in a crate."

"Thanks, Bill."

"I'm going to miss you buddy."

"Look me up when you're in the States," I said. "And send me a postcard once in a while."

Bill agreed to stay for lunch. Afterward we said our good-byes to Henri and Cosette. I owed them so much I didn't know what to say. We kissed cheeks and said *bonne chance*.

Bill told us it would take a few hours to get to the coast.

Zelie looked at me with a mix of anxiety and anticipation. She'd never been on a boat before. I took her hand.

I half expected Remy to show up but I imagined he was eager to get back to his normal life. No need to hide in Marseille anymore. That would make his mother happy.

Bill had thought of everything. He handed me and Zelie a couple of seasickness pills.

On the yacht we were instructed to stay below by the captain, a tall fellow in his 50's who looked like he'd just stepped away from his country club. A friend of Allen Dulles, Bill told me. When we left the port, he knocked on the door and told us we were free to stand on deck.

We were close enough to shore to see Dieppe fading into the channel mist. The colors of France in full display. They were, I realized, the colors of my life with Liana — the tinted colors of her glass tree.

I looked over at Zelie, who was watching the only home she'd ever known disappear. If not forever, at least for the foreseeable future. I needed to be a good father for her. If she was going to believe the world could be a happier place than the one she'd known, I'd have to believe it too. It was going to be hard for both of us. But the girl was strong, she had character, and wouldn't give up. And someday, I hoped, she'd find someone to love as much as I loved my wife.

She caught me looking at her, instead of the distant coast, and put her head against my shoulder. I wrapped my arm around her. I was bringing France, and Liana, home.

Acknowledgements

First, a very special thank you to my dedicated peer readers for their insights along this journey: Ronald Rhault, Jason Mazzarino, Abbey Keith, Emily Manz, Cricket VanAlstyne, and Evan Gregg. Next, a huge thank you to my editor Sara Rauch for her many keen observations and hard work. For sound advice and encouragement along the way, thanks to Scott Smith, Tom Maguire and Lance Bouten. More thanks to Galen Munroe, proof reading extraordinaire and Sabine Charton-Long for getting the French text in this book just right.

Thanks to author Stanley Karnow for his book *Paris in the Fifties* which was very useful for better understanding the political intrigue and charged atmosphere of Paris during the Cold War.